"Yo, Walloper," Gasser Phipps asked out of the blue. "What's that funny-looking thing hanging over your head?"

"What thing?" I said.

"That rubbery black pillow of a thing," Gasser said.

"I don't know what you're talking about," I said, because truly I didn't.

I reached up and felt over my head. I didn't feel anything.

"It's true," insisted the others, staring at me with wide eyes. "Sort of like a shadow, only kind of misty. Definitely weird."

At that my heart sank faster than my batting average. It fell like a piano plunging over a cliff. I didn't need a mirror to know what they were talking about.

I gulped. "It must be a slump."

KEVIN MARKEY

Illustrated by Royce Fitzgerald

HARPER

An Imprint of HarperCollinsPublishers

The Super Sluggers: Slumpbuster

Library of Congress Cataloging-in-Publication Data
Markey, Kevin.
  Slumpbuster / by Kevin Markey ; illustrated by Royce
Fitzgerald. — 1st ed.
    p. cm. — (Super Sluggers)
  Summary: Eleven-year-old slugger Banjo "The Great
Walloper" Bishbash is overcome by a nasty hitting slump as
he tries to lead the Rambletown Rounders to the division
baseball championship.
  ISBN 978-0-06-115220-7
  [1. Baseball—Fiction. 2. Self-confidence—Fiction.]
I. Fitzgerald, Royce, ill. II. Title.
PZ7.M3394546Sl 2009   2008019661
[Fic]—dc22   CIP
                                                    AC

Typography by Larissa Lawrynenko
10 11 12 13 14   LP/CW   10 9 8 7 6 5 4 3 2 1
❖
First paperback edition, 2010

For Brendan, an All-Star

★ CHAPTER 1 ★

"ALL SET, MR. BONES?" I asked.

Mr. Bones didn't say anything. He just ran over to the back door and wagged his tail. He wagged it so hard I thought he might take off into the air like a helicopter. Mr. Bones was my dog, a short-legged, long-nosed, yellow-haired fur ball that strangers often mistook for a bandicoot. He loved baseball. He came to all my games. My teammates thought he brought good luck. I thought they were right.

Mr. Bones wagged some more. All his wagging stirred up a tail wind that blew a newspaper right off the mail table. He was ready, all right.

And so was I.

I was ready to take on the Hog City Haymakers in the biggest game of the year.

I played third base for the Rambletown Rounders. With a week left in the season, we were neck and neck in the standings with the Haymakers, the reigning champs of the 10–12 division. If we could beat our archrivals, we would be in a good position to win the pennant.

Winning would be tough. On top of being good, the Haymakers were big. Really big. Every kid on the team looked like a grown man. I swear some of those bad boys even had mustaches, which was very strange for a bunch of kids who'd be entering sixth grade in the fall. You just didn't see many sixth graders with full handlebar mustaches.

I picked up the newspaper Mr. Bones had wagged to the floor. It was folded open to the sports section. In the middle of the page was a picture of me hitting a home run for the Rounders. The picture was taken by Gabby

Hedron. She was my friend and classmate at Rambletown Elementary. She covered baseball for the *Rambletown Bulletin*. The caption under the picture said:

WALLOPER SET TO SWING INTO ACTION AGAINST HAYMAKERS!
The Rambletown slugger has hit a home run in every game this season. If the pattern holds, he'll launch another one today and catapult the Rounders into first place.

Walloper was what my friends called me. It was short for the Great Walloper, on account of I liked to wallop the tar out of the ball. I got that nickname back in the Pee Wees, when I first started going deep.

My cheeks burned a little bit as I replaced the paper on the table. I made a point of turning it over, picture side down. It was one thing to hit a dinger now and then and another thing for the newspaper to trumpet it all over the universe. I didn't really like being the center of attention. I was just one player. The Rounders were a team. It took a team to win a division crown. Plus, it was just plain bad luck to talk about home runs before they happened. It sounded boastful. What on earth was Gabby thinking?!

I tugged on my blue cap with the red Rambletown *R* on the front, tucked my mitt under my arm, and pulled open the door. Mr. Bones rocketed out of the house like he'd been blasted from a cannon.

"Hold on, boy!" I called from the porch. "We've got plenty of time."

Mr. Bones pulled up short and cocked his head over his shoulder, urging me to get the lead out. He couldn't wait to get to the ballpark. One thing about dogs was that they had no sense of time. When they were ready, they were ready.

I wheeled my bike onto the driveway and hung my mitt on the handlebar. My mom was yanking weeds in her flower garden. When she saw me, she pulled off her gardening gloves and came right over.

"You sure you don't want a ride?" she asked, wiping her forehead with the back of her hand. "It's gotten really hot all of a sudden. The tiger lilies are drooping. Only the weeds seem to be thriving."

I nodded. I always rode my bike to home games. Mr. Bones always trotted along behind. It was a good ritual. I didn't want to mess with it before our showdown with the Haymakers, heat or no heat.

"Good luck then, slugger," Mom said, planting a kiss on the crown of my Rounders cap. "I'll be in the bleachers at the start of the second inning."

That was another one of our rituals. My parents always arrived an inning late. It started a long time ago, when they happened to miss the first inning because my dad couldn't find the car keys. My dad was always misplacing the car keys. But that's another story. In any case, I ended up going four for four with four round-trippers that day. After that, my parents started coming late on purpose. From my position at third base, I often saw them dawdling in the parking lot, killing time until it was safe to grab seats in the bleachers.

"Thanks, Mom," I said.

I mounted my bike and headed for Rambletown Field, Mr. Bones bouncing eagerly at my rear wheel.

"Remember to drink plenty of water, Banjie," my mom called. She and my dad were about the only ones who used my real name. Or at least something like it. My actual name was Banjo.

Banjo H. Bishbash.

The *H* stood for Hit. It was my mother's last name before she married my dad. My parents gave it to me in part to honor her side of the family and in part because my dad loved baseball. "You can't go wrong with a middle name like Hit," he said.

The Banjo didn't stand for anything. It was just Banjo, plain and simple, like the musical instrument. The name came from my grandfather on my dad's side. Gramps got stuck with it first, and my dad got stuck with it after him. If I ever have a kid, I may just break the trend and call him something normal. "Mike" has a nice solid ring to it. According to family history, my grandfather was so long and skinny when he was born, with such a big head, that his folks took one look and called him Banjo. I guess it could've been worse. They could've called him Lollipop or Stop Sign.

In any case, it wasn't hard to see why I preferred Walloper.

★ CHAPTER 2 ★

A FIVE-MINUTE RIDE over the smooth sidewalks of Rambletown brought me and Mr. Bones to the field. The first thing I noticed after leaning my bike against the fence was that pregame warm-ups were in full swing. I was glad to see my teammates had all arrived early. It meant they were as pumped for the game as I was.

Skipper Lou "Skip-to-My-Lou" Clementine was knocking balls around the diamond from home plate. Skipper Lou was our manager. During the school year, he taught music at Rambletown Elementary. Played a mean clarinet. The door to his office said MR. CLEMENTINE.

But to kids on the Rounders he would always be Skipper Lou Skip-to-My-Lou. Skip Lou for short. He knew everything there was to know about baseball.

The second thing I noticed was that Rambletown Field was looking kind of raggedy. Patches of normally lush outfield grass were turning brown under the withering sun and the base paths looked all puckery, like your lips felt after you ate too much popcorn. When Skip Lou smacked a grounder, the ball kicked up a comet trail of dust as it skittered across the parched infield.

"Looks like the dog days of summer have arrived with a vengeance," I said, adding, "no offense, Mr. Bones."

I gave my dog a pat, then slipped my hand

into my tan leather glove. Mr. Bones loped into the dugout and stretched out in the shade under the aluminum bench. As I jogged out toward third base, someone called my name. Turning, I saw Gabby Hedron waving from behind the backstop.

Gabby had a camera on a black strap looped around her neck and carried a small notebook. Her long brown ponytail stuck out through the opening at the back of the Rounders cap she wore. So much for the press not taking sides.

"You going to hit a homer today, Walloper?" she called.

Remembering the photo in the morning paper, I turned red as a tomato.

"No one can predict home runs," I shouted back. "We'll just have to play the game and see what happens."

"Well, I can predict them. It's easy, because you always hit at least one. In fact, I already pretty much said in the paper that you would. Did you see the story?"

"I saw it all right," I said.

"Great shot, wasn't it?"

"I've got to go," I said curtly.

"Don't let me down, Walloper!"

I ducked my head and charged onto the field, hoping no one had noticed me talking to Gabby. Or blushing. When I looked up, shortstop Stump Plumwhiff caught my eye. He was grinning like a cat with a mouse under its paw. I knew I was in for it.

"Ooh, Walloper, hit a home run for me," he teased, making goo-goo eyes. "My hero!"

My friend Stump was a funny kid. He had red hair that stuck straight up like rooster feathers when he took off his baseball cap. For this reason, he almost never took it off. He even slept in it. I knew that for a fact, because we often had sleepovers. We'd been friends forever and had played baseball together for just as long. We were both eleven. In the fall, we would start sixth grade at Rambletown Middle School.

"She doesn't know what she's talking about," I sputtered, a little bit too loudly. "She's crazy."

As soon as I said it, I felt bad. Gabby was a great girl. She was nuts for the Rounders, but she wasn't crazy. Crazy was shaving your hair off and painting your bald head in team colors and banging a giant gong in the bleachers while you heckled the other team. Gabby didn't do any of those things. She was too cool for that. I glanced over at her. She was staring at me and Stump. When she saw me looking, she quickly turned away.

"Seriously, dude, I'm just glad you could finally make it," Stump said, changing the subject but still needling me. "I was beginning to think you'd decided to take a rain check."

A real rain check would have been nice. It would've meant rain. A nice thunderstorm would have cooled down the hot day.

"You're kidding, right?" I called back. "You know I wouldn't miss this one for a million bucks. You psyched as I am?"

"You know it! I can't wait to hand these guys their hats—they're so cocky!"

Without warning, Skip Lou cracked a screamer my way. I dived to my left and snatched the line drive out of the air like I was picking an apple from a tree. Bouncing up quickly, I fired the ball to Gilly Wishes at first. He stepped on the bag and tossed the pill to the catcher, Tugboat Tooley, who fed it back to Skip.

It felt good to snare that first one. Nothing like fielding a sharp liner at the "hot corner," which is what we called third base, to get your mind in the game.

Skip continued driving the ball around the field. He mixed up his hits, slapping bouncers around the infield, driving flies to the outfield. Every player got a chance to make a catch and show off his throwing arm.

As we practiced, the Haymakers began arriving. They marched into our park like they owned the place, gathering on the first baseline to watch us. They wore fancy blue-and-white pinstripe uniforms and sour looks on their faces. Strictly speaking, scowls were not part of the Hog City uniform. But they might as well have been, rare as it was that you ever saw a Haymaker smile.

It wasn't long before the visitors started cracking on us. Standing out at third, I couldn't hear exactly what they were saying. But I could tell from their snickers that it wasn't friendly banter. That was the thing about the Haymakers. They were as mean as they were supersized. Maybe even meaner.

The Haymakers didn't just like to beat teams; they liked to stomp them. They would do anything to get a leg up on you. When sliding into base, they always came at you feet high and spikes gleaming. Thinking about those spikes could make you lose concentration and drop the ball. Often they slid even when there was no play at the base. They just got a kick out of making you flinch.

Even worse was when one of them smashed a home run. If you happened to be playing infield and a Haymaker knocked a ball into the stands, look out! He would stomp your foot as he tore around the bases. If you made the mistake of complaining, he would just laugh. Unfortunately, the Haymakers hit home runs like fishermen catch fish—by the boatload.

That's the kind of team the Haymakers were. Big. Mean. And unstoppable. They hadn't lost in two years. But we needed to take them down now. If we did, we would have the inside track on the pennant. And the pennant was what all of us Rounders really wanted. We craved it like bears crave honey. Every season we seemed to come close, only to lose out to the Haymakers. We were tired of being second best. We wanted to win the whole shooting match for once. And now, with the season winding down, the pennant was so close we could almost touch it.

But first we had to get past the Haymakers.

From the sideline, the visitors' cackles grew louder.

"Call that an arm?" One of them hooted when our left fielder, Ducks Bunion, bounced a short throw to second. "That's no arm. It's a wet noodle. My grandmother can throw harder than that!"

"Your infield is like a sieve! It lets everything through."

"You should get some frogs to play outfield. They're better at catching flies than you chumps."

The insults began to get under our skin. All of a sudden, we started booting balls like the game was soccer instead of baseball. Muffing grounders. Dropping easy pop-ups. We looked like a bunch of rookies. It was unsettling. The game hadn't even started yet and already the Haymakers were beating us like a drum.

When I let a soft roller skip through my legs, Skip Lou had seen enough.

"Bring it in, fellows," he called from home

plate. "This clearly isn't going anywhere."

To the howls of the Haymakers, we slunk off the field, heads hanging low.

"In the dugout, everybody," Skip Lou ordered. "Grab a drink and grab a seat."

One by one, we filled paper cups from a cooler of ice water and took our places on the long bench. Mr. Bones was glad for the company. He crawled out from under the bench and rolled over to have his belly scratched, his tail wagging a mile a minute. At the moment, he was the only one in the dugout who was feeling any kind of happy.

"Listen up, guys," Skip Lou began, pacing back and forth across the concrete floor like a general in his bunker. "You can't let the Haymakers rattle you. If they're going to win the game, let's at least make them do it on the diamond. Sure, they're big, and sure, they can be kind of mouthy. But you know what? None of that matters. Because this is baseball, and the only thing that counts is the game and how you play it. I want you guys just to be yourselves. Go out there and have fun and play the way I know you can. If you do that, everything will be fine. Now, how about we show some of that old Rounders spirit!"

Revved up by his pep talk, we charged out of the dugout and took our positions under the blazing afternoon sun.

"PLAY BALL!" roared the umpire.

The game started.

It started badly.

Really badly.

★ CHAPTER 3 ★

ALL THE HAYMAKERS WERE big, but the first one to come to the plate was larger than life. He was the size of my mom's minivan. He had to be at least thirteen. Maybe even older. His arms bulged like the Incredible Hulk's. It looked like there were pumpkins stuffed inside the sleeves of his jersey. He should have been playing in a different league for a different team. Like maybe the New York Yankees.

"C'mon now, Slingshot," I called to our pitcher, Slocum. "Whip it past him. He's got nothing."

Easy for me to say.

Slingshot reared back and fired the game's

first pitch. Fastball. A good one that dived toward the outside corner as it hurtled homeward. The giant flicked his bat like a snake flicks its tongue. He slapped the ball into right field for a single. As he rumbled down the line, he turned and taunted Slingshot.

"Some fastball," he sneered. "I've seen faster snails."

When he got to the bag, he stomped on the foot of Gilly Wishes, our hard-nosed first baseman.

Gilly winced, but he didn't say anything. That made the runner mad.

"Next time it'll be even harder, squirt," he growled.

"That's enough of that," snapped the umpire. "Just play ball, guys."

Gilly tossed the ball back to Slingshot. The next overgrown Haymaker dug in at the plate.

Slingshot wound up and delivered a looping curve. Most batters would have been frozen stiffer than an icicle by the big hook, but it didn't

21

bother the Haymaker batter one bit. He coolly tattooed it up the middle. Our second baseman, Ellis "the Glove" Rodriguez, dived for it. Too late. The ball bounded into center field for a hit.

With runners on first and second, Slingshot called time and stepped off the mound. He mopped his face with his sleeve. He was a great pitcher. He was also smart, maybe the smartest kid in Mrs. Decker's class last year. Two things you could count on from Slingshot: strikeouts and straight As. Most of the time, anyway.

He climbed back up the hill.

Waiting at the plate was Flicker Pringle, the Haymakers' star pitcher and best all-around player.

Slingshot stared home, peering under the bill of his cap to get the call from our catcher, Tugboat Tooley.

Tugboat flashed one finger, the signal for a fastball.

Slingshot nodded.

"You planning on throwing the ball, or you just going to stand there playing peekaboo with your catcher all day?" Flicker hooted.

Slingshot didn't so much as raise an eyebrow in response. Without a word, he wound up and busted a heater in tight on Flicker's hands. It was an almost perfect pitch.

Any ordinary hitter would have been lucky to foul it off. Most would have swung right through it. Either way it was a strike.

But Flicker Pringle was no ordinary batter.

Quick as a mongoose, the big right-hander turned on the ball and parked it over the left-field wall.

Just like that, three runs scored.

This was definitely not how we wanted to start the game.

"Settle down now, Slingshot," I called as the next batter came up. "You can get this guy. Just pitch your game."

With a face as serious as a gunslinger's, Slingshot kicked high and delivered the pitch.

The batter swung a hair late and missed by just that much: a hair.

"That's the stuff, ace," shouted Skip Lou from the dugout.

"Lucky is all that was," grumbled the batter.

It wasn't luck though. Not at all. It was talent and hard work and smarts.

Getting that first strike settled Slingshot down. He began to find his rhythm. Using his brain and his arm, he threw every kind of pitch he could think of. Inside ones, outside ones, fast ones, slow ones. Bloopers that dropped into the catcher's mitt like little red-stitched parachutes, submariners that zipped in low like torpedoes. For the rest of the inning his stuff was too good for the Haymakers. He struck out three batters in a row and made them look bad doing it.

After the third out, we jogged off the field feeling a little better about our chances. Slingshot had dug deep. He had shown courage. He had held the mighty Haymakers to three runs. Now we had to get to work at the plate.

Against Flicker Pringle we knew the job wouldn't be easy. He was the scariest fastballer in the league. The moment he released the ball, it seemed to zoom past you. It was like he placed it directly in the catcher's mitt. Getting a hit off him was like trying to make two plus two add up to five.

But we sure were going to try.

"BATTER UP!" barked the umpire.

Ducks Bunion, our left fielder, stepped to the plate.

When Ducks was little, they say, he waddled from side to side while learning to walk. Which was how he got his nickname. Patrolling left field and running the bases for the Rounders, he was as fleet as a cheetah.

Flicker Pringle glowered down from the mound. He looked ten feet tall up there, his arms as long as fire hoses.

"Watch out, Ducks," snarled the Haymaker catcher, Hanky Burns. "He's going to stick the first one in your ear."

"He wouldn't," exclaimed Ducks, his eyes widening.

"Oh, he would all right," said Hanky. "You know Flicker's nasty that way."

Flicker reached back and fired a lightning

bolt. Spooked by Hanky's taunt, Ducks hit the dirt.

"STEEE-RIKE!" called the umpire. "Right down the middle."

Out on the mound, Flicker Pringle rolled his trademark toothpick from one side of his mouth to the other. It was as close as he ever came to smiling. Ducks looked so embarrassed, I bet all he wanted to do was get back to the bench and hide his face. It took Flicker Pringle exactly two more pitches to gas him.

Then he fanned Stump.

Then it was my turn.

★ CHAPTER 4 ★

BILLY WISHES, OUR BATBOY, handed me my favorite Louisville Slugger.

"Thanks, Billy," I said. "Did you give it a good rub?"

"Extragood," said Billy.

Billy was the kid brother of our first baseman, Gilly. He was too young to play for the Rounders, but we loved having him around. For one thing, he was always cheerful. For another, he was luckier than a field of four-leaf clovers. He was always finding cool stuff and winning prizes. One time Billy and his mom were leaving a store, and bells and lights started going off like crazy. The manager came running over, and Mrs.Wishes thought she was in trouble. But the manager said Billy was the one-millionth customer and the store was celebrating by sending him to Walt Disney World. The whole family went to Florida for a week, and Billy got his picture in the paper.

With luck like that, we figured it made sense to keep Billy around. Maybe some of it would rub off on us.

I strode up to the plate. I tried to feel brave.

Out on the mound, Flicker Pringle glared at me like I'd eaten the last cookie in the box. The one he'd been saving for himself. His eyes were hot and smoky, like the eyes of some kind of demon. He wound up and threw the ball. At least I think he did. He whipped it so fast, I never saw it.

I heard it, though.

The ball *whoosh*ed like a steam engine. Then came a firecracker pop as it slammed into the catcher's mitt. Next was a sharp yelp that sounded like Mr. Bones when he got underfoot

and I accidentally stepped on his paw.

The yelp came from the catcher, Hanky Burns.

It hurt to catch Flicker Pringle's hard pitches. Even the toughest catchers could only take an inning or two of it. That old fireballer went through catchers like a person with a cold goes through tissues.

"STEE-RIKE ONE," the umpire yelled.

Flicker scowled down at me, rolling the toothpick around in his mouth. I knew he was laughing at me—which made me mad. When the next pitch came, I swung hard enough to turn the ball inside out. I would have, too. If only I had hit it.

WHOOSH! went the ball.

"YOWCH!" cried Hanky Burns.

"STEE-RIKE TWO!" barked the umpire.

"Not even close," hissed Flicker Pringle. He had a voice like a rattlesnake, if rattlesnakes had voices.

From the bench, Skipper Lou shouted encouragement. "Next one's yours, Walloper," he said. "Dig in now and clock it to Kalamazoo!"

I clapped my helmet down tight and waited for the fastball I knew was coming. When it did, I swung like my dad when he made one of his famous overstuffed omelets. I put everything into it. And I missed the ball like you miss a school bus. It just passed me right by.

"YOU'RE OUT!" bellowed the umpire.

Poor Hanky Burns lay whimpering on the ground. With a heavy heart, I stepped over him and trudged back to the dugout.

Way out in the bleachers, fans stood and cheered.

"What are they so happy about?" I asked Skip Lou.

"Well, Walloper," he said, "I believe they are grateful for the breath of air. You whiffed so hard you stirred up a nice cooling breeze that carried all the way out to the cheap seats. Between the heat and the way this game is going, it's the only thing our fans have to feel good about."

With that, we took the field for the top of the second inning.

Slingshot climbed the hill and did his best impersonation of a tent. He pitched. With all his heart, he pitched.

The first Haymaker of the second inning popped weakly to Gasser Phipps in short center field. Haymaker number two snarled and grunted and piffled a lazy grounder to short. Stump hoovered it cleanly and fired to Gilly at first for the second out.

The third guy up surprised us all by dropping a bunt down the third baseline. My line. I wasn't ready for it at all. By the time I scooped up the ball and made the long throw across the diamond, the runner was already standing safely on first, one cleat planted firmly on Gilly's left foot.

Slingshot got the ball back and nodded my way.

"Forget about it, Walloper," he said. "Nobody would have expected a bunt."

He doused the threat by striking out the next Haymaker on three straight changeups. The pitches moved so slowly, and fooled the batter so completely, that he actually swung twice at the last one. Fortunately for us, he missed both times.

"Way to go, Slingshot," I said, laughing. "Four strikes on three pitches. You sure don't see that every day."

Our joy didn't last very long. Trotting off the roasting-hot field was pretty much like going from the frying pan into the fire.

The fire was Flicker Pringle.

The Haymaker ace picked up in the second right where he'd left off in the first—blazing fastballs straight past us. He was so good, and we were so lousy, the umpire started to sound like a broken record. He just said the same thing over and over:

"STEE-RIKE ONE!
STEE-RIKE TWO!
STEE-RIKE THREE! YOU'RE OUT!"

"STEE-RIKE ONE!
STEE-RIKE TWO!

STEE-RIKE THREE! YOU'RE OUT!"

"STEE-RIKE ONE!
STEE-RIKE TWO!
STEE-RIKE THREE! YOU'RE OUT!"

It reached the point where I began to feel bad for the poor ump. Probably he would have traded his whisk brush just for the chance to say "FOUL BALL!" Anything other than "STEE-RIKE!"

But stingy old Flicker Pringle didn't give him the opportunity. He turned baseball into bowling, where he was the bowling ball and the Rounders were pins. He set us down one after another.

Before we knew it, the second inning was over and we were back out on the field.

I didn't come up again until there were two outs in the fourth inning. The score was still 3–0, Haymakers on top. I hoped to change all that with one swing of my trusty Louisville Slugger.

35

"Go get 'em, Walloper," said Billy Wishes, handing me the bat.

"I'm sure going to try," I said, rubbing his head for extra luck.

"BATTER UP!" roared the umpire.

★ CHAPTER 5 ★

I COCKED THE BAT OVER my shoulder.

Zoom went the pitch.

Whoosh fanned my swing.

"Yowch!" griped the substitute catcher, fresh meat who'd come in for Hanky Burns in the third. Hanky sat on the bench with his hand plunged into a tub of ice. Between the cold ice and being finished catching Flicker for the day, he was the happiest guy at the ballpark.

"STEE-RIKE ONE!" roared the umpire.

"I've heard that before," I said, and dug in for Flicker Pringle's second offering.

I caught a glimpse of the next pitch as it zipped toward me. A quick peek. At least I think

I did. Either that, or what I saw was a mirage caused by the shimmering heat. In any case, it disappeared in a flash. I swung hard. And missed by a mile.

"STEE-RIKE TWO!" bellowed the ump.

On the mound, Flicker rolled his toothpick to the side of his mouth. He was feeling pretty pleased with himself.

"I'm going to make this next one easy for you, Walloper," he jeered.

"How's that?" I asked.

"I'm going to tell you exactly what's coming. Fastball. Right over the fat part of the plate."

A big gasp swept through the bleachers as the crowd sucked in its breath all at once. The fans couldn't believe Flicker Pringle was taunting me. I couldn't believe it either.

A lone voice fractured the stunned silence. It was Gabby Hedron, and she was hopping mad.

"You're asking for it now, mister," she threatened from the press box, along the third baseline. "Teach him some manners, Walloper. Knock that ball out of here!"

I wiped my sweaty palms on my pants, then dug in at the plate.

"Bring it." I bristled.

With that, Flicker whistled one down the middle. Just like he said he would.

Whoosh went my swing.

"Yowch!" yelped the catcher.

"STEE-RIKE THREE!" barked the umpire. "YOU'RE OUT!"

"Don't you ever get tired of saying that?" I asked, before plodding back to the dugout.

In the bleachers, fans leaned back and basked in my breeze. It wasn't a hit and it wouldn't win the game, but at least it took the edge off the miserable heat.

The fifth inning passed without either team scoring. We did get two runners on base in our half. Slingshot made it to first when the Haymaker catcher dropped a hot third strike and the ball rolled all the way to the backstop.

Flicker Pringle got so mad about the mistake that he drilled Ocho in the hip with the very next pitch. The umpire gave him a warning, and our modest threat expired when the Glove went down swinging at invisible fastballs.

We entered the sixth and final frame still down by three runs. Slingshot did his job in the top half, retiring the Haymakers in order. His work done for the day, he walked off the mound to a standing ovation from the Rambletown faithful, who knew how hard it was to hold the powerful Haymakers to three measly runs.

Any chance at victory lay with our hitters. We needed to do some damage against Flicker Pringle.

The Glove led off with a soft grounder that found a crack of daylight between short and third and dribbled into left field for a single. Ducks strode to the plate. On the bench, we turned our caps around backward and linked our arms for a rally.

If Flicker was nervous, he didn't show it. He

blew a first-pitch fastball past Ducks, then got him to loft a pop into foul territory behind home. Throwing off his mask, the catcher sprang to his feet. The ball settled into his mitt like a bird coming home to nest. One out.

Stump came up and worked the count full.

"Good eye!" we hollered from the bench. "Wait for your pitch."

His pitch never came, though. Flicker caught him looking on a curve over the outside corner. Two outs. We were still alive, but barely.

The fans didn't even bother to cheer when they saw me coming. They just tilted back their heads, spread their arms wide, and waited for the breeze. I tried to ignore them. I knew I could get us right back into the game with one swing of the bat. On the other hand, if I made an out, the game would be over. A Haymakers win.

I took a couple practice swings and waited for the pitch.

I didn't have to wait long. Flicker's windup

was faster than instant oatmeal. And the pitch he hurled at me was even less appetizing.

"STEE-RIKE ONE!" roared the ump.

"Come on, now, Walloper," bawled Skip Lou. "One pitch. One is all you need, buddy!"

Flicker rolled his eyes, then he rolled his toothpick from one side of his mouth to the other. Laughing at me again. As he went into his windup, the Glove took off for second. Flicker didn't even bother to check him. His thinking was as clear as a freshly washed window: Why worry about a base runner when he could fan me like a bowl of hot soup?

He kicked and delivered. I waved at the pitch as it barreled past, an express train that left me stranded at the station.

"STEE-RIKE TWO!" bellowed the umpire.

"Here you go, kid, one pitch," called Stump gamely from the bench. "Make this one yours, Walloper."

His voice was the only sound at Rambletown Field. The fans who hadn't left already were as still as statues, stunned by too much sun and too few hits.

Flicker Pringle reached back and busted another fastball. Out of the corner of my eye, I saw the Glove digging for third. What I didn't see was the ball.

"STEE-RIKE THREE!" roared the ump. "YOU'RE OUT!"

"You don't have to rub it in," I muttered. "I know I'm out. Out of strikes, out of hits, and out of luck."

Dragging my bat behind me, I trudged back to the dugout. All around me, Haymakers whooped and slapped high-fives. It was terrible to see them celebrating on our own field.

The Rounders slouched on the bench, sipping ice water. Nobody talked much. We all felt pretty glum. Even Mr. Bones did. That dog didn't so much as lick anyone's face. We'd lost the game, we were stuck in second place, and it was all my fault. Three trips to the plate, three strikeouts. I was stunned. I'd never had an oh-fer day at the plate in my life. It made me want to puke. Truth be told, it scared me, too. Hitting was supposed to be easy for me. Always had been. "Hit" was my middle name, after all. And here I'd gone oh for three in the biggest game of the year. What was my problem? Had I been done in by the hot weather? I wondered. The blazing sun and air felt as gooey as molasses. I wasn't used to this kind of heat. But then again, neither was anybody else. The strange weather sure hadn't sapped Flicker Pringle any.

I was sitting there feeling as shaken as a pair of maracas when Gasser Phipps looked my way.

"Yo, Walloper. What's that funny-looking thing hanging over your head?" he asked out of the blue.

"What thing?" I said.

"That rubbery black pillow of a thing," Gasser said.

"I don't know what you're talking about," I said, because truly I didn't. I reached up and felt over my head. I didn't feel anything.

"It's true," insisted the others, staring at me with wide eyes. "Sort of like a shadow, only kind of misty. Definitely weird."

At that my heart sank faster than my batting

average. It fell like a piano plunging over a cliff. I didn't need a mirror to know what they were talking about.

"It must be a slump." I gulped.

I'd heard about hitting slumps taking on lives of their own, getting so deep and sorrowful that you could actually see them. But up until that moment I'd never really believed it could happen. And now I had one, hanging over my head for everyone to see.

A stone-cold silence fell over the dugout. The coldest silence on the hottest day on record.

★ CHAPTER 6 ★

IFELT SO LOW-DOWN and blue that only one thing would help: fried-baloney sandwiches. It was a tradition in our family. When things got bad, we started sizzling up baloney and toasting bread. I highly recommend it.

Sure enough, Mom was standing over the stove, cooking up a storm, when Mr. Bones and I got home.

"Oh, honey," she said as we came through the doorway. That's all she said. Usually she talked a lot. This time she didn't have to say anything. We both understood.

When the sandwiches were done, Mom piled them up on a big white platter. She carried it to the kitchen table and set down a bottle of ketchup beside it. Mr. Bones came over and put his paws up on my chest and licked my face. I shared supper with him. A fried-baloney sandwich for me, a fried-baloney sandwich for Mr. Bones.

While we were munching and chewing, my dad came home from work.

"Hungry?" I asked as he dropped into a chair next to me, panting from the heat outside. I grabbed a fried-baloney sandwich off the stack and waved it at him.

"No thanks, sport." He shook his head. "You enjoy them. I've got no appetite. I could drink the entire Rambletown Reservoir, though." He patted my shoulder gently. "You'll get those Haymakers next time." He patted me on the shoulder again before getting up and kissing my mom. Usually he pats my head, but I guess my slump got in his way.

"I've never seen anything like it," I heard him mutter.

"Honey, sssshh!" Mom said sharply. "It's only one game."

"Game?" Dad asked. "Oh, right. Banjie's game. No, I was talking about the weather. I've never seen anything like it. You know that big fountain over on Maple Street? When I drove past, a whole family had set up camp there."

"Swimming?" I asked.

49

"No, cooking spaghetti. The water was actually boiling! That's how steamy it is."

"Oh, the heat," Mom said. "I'm sure it'll pass. It's summer, after all. I just hope you know what else does, too."

"You know what *what*?" Dad asked. "What do I know *what*? You know I can't think straight when it's this hot."

"She's talking about my slump," I explained between mouthfuls. Sometimes Dad can be pretty clueless. "It's okay, Mom. You can say it. I mean, we can't exactly pretend it's not there. Especially since it's hovering over me like the Goodyear blimp."

"It is not like a blimp," Mom said sternly. "You can hardly even notice it, for pete's sake."

"Is that what that horrible thing is?" Dad said. "A hitting slump? I was afraid to ask. I thought that maybe you'd gone and gotten a ridiculous haircut, some rock-star kind of thing to impress girls. It looks like a mushroom cloud."

"Dad!" I said.

"What? It's not so bad. I've seen worse slumps."

"Really? Where?" If there ever had been a slump worse than mine, I sure wanted to hear about it.

"Oh, one summer when I was a boy. Kid on my baseball team got into such a bad slump, fire trucks started showing up wherever he went. Sirens, bells, flashing lights, the works. Dalmatians. Thing was, people saw his slump and right away they thought it was smoke. Poor kid couldn't make a trip to the refrigerator without someone calling the fire department."

"What was his name?"

"Funny," Dad said. He scratched his head. "For the life of me I can't remember his real name. We called him Five-Alarm Ferguson."

"Five-Alarm Ferguson!" I yelped. "That doesn't exactly make me feel a whole lot better."

"Nice work, dear," Mom said. She swatted Dad with a dish towel. "Five-Alarm Ferguson!"

But she was giggling. I guess Dad's silly story made me laugh a little bit, too, but not enough to lay off the old fried-baloney sandwiches.

Mr. Bones and I kept at it until we had eaten our way clean through a pound of baloney and a whole loaf of Old Leadbelly Sinker Bread. Then I put my plate in the dishwasher and started to go upstairs to clean up.

"Game of pepper before you hit the shower?" Dad asked. "It's still light. I could toss you a few."

"Thanks, Dad. Not tonight."

"That's fine, sport. Another time."

Mom wrapped me up in a big hug. "Things will be better in the morning, honey. You'll see."

I sure hoped she was right.

★ CHAPTER 7 ★

ALL NIGHT LONG I dreamed of invisible fast-balls I couldn't hit because I couldn't see.

I don't know what Mr. Bones dreamed about, but it might have been fried-baloney sandwiches. All night long, his stomach rumbled, his lips smacked, and his farts ripped through the room like dynamite.

In the morning, I rolled out of bed, hoping for the best. I jumped in the shower and avoided looking in the mirror afterward. I couldn't bear to see if my slump was still up there. Everything seemed fine until I put on my uniform for a doubleheader against the Lumleyville Lumberjacks. As I pulled my jersey

over my head, it snagged on my slump. Not
good. Not good at all. Feeling rottener than
ever, I went down for breakfast.

"How about a nice omelet?" my dad offered.
He loved to make omelets. They were his spe-
cialty. An omelet was a joyful thing for him. It
was more than breakfast; it was a party in a
pan.

But I wasn't in the mood. Not with that foul
slump in the air.

"Not today, Dad. Just cereal, I think."

Looking disappointed, he took a box of
Pirate Crunch from the cupboard.

The Pirate Crunch cereal was the kind with frosted cannonballs, those round little marshmallow puffs. When I added milk to the bowl, the cannonballs dipped and bobbed in the bowl. They looked like dozens of tiny baseballs. It made my head spin to see them. I could never hit all those baseballs, not with the slump I was in.

"On second thought, maybe I will have that omelet," I said, pushing away the bowl.

Dad's face lit up like a lamp.

"Now you're talking, sport!" He beamed. "Sit tight. This won't take a minute!"

Instantly, he swung into action, lighting the gas under a big frying pan and gathering ingredients from the fridge. He seemed to crack eggs, chop vegetables, and grate cheese all at the same time, arms waving so swiftly he could have been an octopus conducting an orchestra.

My mom came into the kitchen in the middle of the performance.

"Oh, no!" she said.

"Oh, yes!" he said.

Sensing the excitement, or maybe smelling eggs and melting cheese, Mr. Bones ran over to his food bowl and looked inside. It was empty.

I'd forgotten to feed him.

"Hold on, buddy," I said, getting up from the table. I poured my soggy cereal into his bowl. "Knock yourself out."

He wagged his tail as though he'd just won the lottery, if dogs had lotteries. He slurped up all the Pirate Crunch cereal, little white cannonball puffs and all.

"Voilà!" said my dad, setting down a steaming omelet. "Eat up, champ. There's hits in omelets. Guaranteed."

I dug in. Ham, cheese, tomato, red and green peppers. Delicious.

"Who's cleaning up the mess?" Mom sighed, pouring herself a cup of coffee. It looked as if a small bomb had gone off in the kitchen. Dishes, spatulas, measuring cups, mixing bowls, knives, and cutting boards of various sizes lay strewn about the counter.

"Sorry," I said between bites. "Doubleheader in Lumleyville. I'm going to have to hurry to catch the bus."

"Leave it, hon," said my dad. "I'll take care of it later." He turned to me. "Need a ride to the park? I can drop you off on my way to work."

"Thanks, but I'll walk," I said. I always walked to the park to catch the team bus for away games. Mr. Bones always came with me. It was a ritual. I couldn't risk breaking it, not with the slump and all.

"Weatherman says it's going to be another scorcher."

"I don't mind."

"This weather reminds me of that heat wave we had when I was a kid. It got so hot and dry the post office had to suspend mail delivery."

"I thought the mail got delivered no matter how horrible the weather. Ran, snow, sleet, drought."

"Oh, it wasn't the weather exactly. It was

that no one could bear the thought of licking an envelope. There just wasn't enough spit to go around."

I think he was making it up. Sometimes with my dad, you couldn't be sure.

"Good luck, slugger." He punched my shoulder lightly and began backing toward the door.

"Before you go, honey, have you seen this morning's *Bulletin*?" my mom asked.

My dad made like a Popsicle and froze. A real Popsicle would have been nice. It would have been cold.

"Uh, yeah, I read it," he stammered. "I mean, I didn't really read it. I looked at it. Where did I put it?"

"Uh, Dad." I laughed. "You're holding it in your left hand. You know, the one behind your back?"

He could be forgetful.

"Holy smokes, am I?" He looked surprised. "So I am!" He tossed the tightly rolled newspaper on the counter like it had bitten him. "I don't even know why we subscribe to this rag. There's nothing in it. Well, so long." He turned quickly and darted out the door.

"That was strange," Mom said as I carried my breakfast plate to the sink. "Is it my imagination, or was he trying to hide the newspaper?"

"Why would Dad hide the newspaper?"

I rinsed my plate and put it in the dishwasher. Then I filled my water bottle and took my insulated lunch box out of the refrigerator. Inside were two peanut-butter-and-jelly sandwiches, carrots sticks, and a small bag of pretzels. It's what I always had for lunch on road trips.

"I think the heat really is getting to him. Oh, well. Good luck today, Banjie. I've got a good feeling. I've got a feeling you're going to rain hits all over those Lumberjacks."

"Sure," I said. "Today's the day."

I gave her a hug. Then I stuffed my glove, my lunch, my water bottle, and a Frisbee into my backpack and headed off with Mr. Bones. The Frisbee was for Mr. Bones to drink out of during the game. It fit into my pack a whole lot better than his water dish.

I wished there was a cure for slumps. I would have stuffed that in there, too.

★ CHAPTER 8 ★

MY DAD WASN'T KIDDING about the weather. If anything, it was already hotter than the day before. Muggier, too. Walking across town felt like wading through a swamp. My slump only made things worse. It was beginning to feel moist and warm itself. I felt as though I was wearing a half-baked cake for a hat.

But the attention I got as Mr. Bones and I raced down the sidewalks of Rambletown told me the thing above my head looked even worse than it felt. Grown men stopped and stared. Mothers pulled children inside from front porches and yards and driveways. They slammed doors and bolted them. You could see pale little faces peeking from behind curtains, mouths hanging open. At the corner of Winterberry and Birch, a delivery van veered into a lamppost while trying to avoid the great blackness. I was a one-person natural disaster.

By the time we got to Rambletown Field, I was drenched in sweat and Mr. Bones was like a clothing store: He was full of pants.

We climbed aboard the idling bus, Skip Lou at the wheel, and started down the aisle to our usual seats in the back. The top of my slump rubbed against the ceiling. All of a sudden, the noisy conversation that normally filled the team bus stopped cold.

"Morning, Stump. Hey, Gilly," I said as I passed my friends. "Let's get a couple Ws today."

Stump stared straight ahead, baseball cap pulled down tight over his carrot-colored hair. He nodded quickly without looking at me or saying a word. Gilly turned and gazed out the window as if the Rambletown Field parking lot was the most fascinating sight in the world.

Mr. Bones and I moved on down the aisle.

"Hey there, Slingshot. Nice pitching yesterday. Too bad we wasted it. We'll get 'em next
time."

Slingshot kept his nose buried in the book
he was reading.

"What's the word, Ducks?" I saluted Ducks
Bunion.

Ducks did not return my greeting.

Not one of my teammates did. They all kept
their mouths shut as tightly as if free speech
cost a dollar and they didn't have the money to
pay. It was as if I'd turned invisible. That's what
a slump does to you.

Skip Lou pulled the lever that closed the bus
door. "Next stop, Lumleyville," he called as we
rattled away from the lot under a big cloud of
dust.

All along the road, wilted cornstalks leaned
against each other for support. Brown pastures
looked sad and lonely, strangely empty in the

shimmering heat. The cows didn't dare leave the shade of their barns. If they had, their milk would've dried up and turned to dust. I bet powdered milk was invented in a heat wave just like this one. I wouldn't recommend it to anyone.

After a while, I got tired of looking at the same dull scenery. What we needed was some entertainment to pass the time. Usually on bus trips somebody brought a GamePod and we all took turns playing stuff like Crash Bam Skateboard Jam and Super Hero House of Horrors. Sometimes Skip Lou passed around his MP3 player. He had it packed full of jazz music. Some of the stuff was actually pretty good—even the songs with clarinets.

"How about some Wacky Banana Ball?" I asked. "Anybody bring a GamePod? Glove?"

Silence.

"Okay, forget the GamePod. How about a deck of cards?"

Card games were an old favorite on the bus. Coming home from a weekend tournament one time, Tugboat and Gasser played an epic game of War. They kept getting into quadruple wars. Gasser finally won, but it took him about three states to do it. Lately, we'd been trying to learn poker. We played for peanuts. Literally. Right fielder Octavio "Ocho" James always packed a jar of them with his lunch.

Nothing.

I was about as popular with the guys as a case of poison ivy.

The cold shoulder hurt me plenty. It hurt Mr. Bones even worse. He was not a dog who liked to be ignored. He was a dog who liked to be petted and liked to lick faces. Getting ignored made him like the old suede shoes that fat guy used to sing about. Elvis Presley.

It made him blue.

Finally, I couldn't take a minute more of it.

"This is bunk," I blurted out. "That's what this is. Bunk. You guys can cold shoulder me all you want. I guess I've got it coming on account of my terrible slump. But can't you at least leave Mr. Bones out of it? He's just a short-legged, long-nosed, yellow-haired fur ball who likes to be petted and likes to lick faces. You guys should be ashamed."

"Aw, cold shoulder nothing," called Stump, breaking the team silence. "I guess you haven't seen it yet."

"All I've seen is my friends and teammates pretending they don't see me. Or hear me. You'd think I stopped existing just because I stopped hitting."

Stump sighed. "You still have it, Rabbit?" He asked over his shoulder. "Show it to him. Go on, do it."

Quiet Kid Rabbit Winkle, our substitute infielder, reluctantly got to his feet. He shuffled down the aisle staring hard at his sneakers, a newspaper clutched in his right hand. He pushed it under my nose.

I looked at it and gasped. All of a sudden my stomach felt more scrambled than eggs. Splashed across the front page of the *Rambletown Bulletin* sports section was a big-as-life picture of me fanning in yesterday's game.

Gabby's caption said:

**WOEFUL WALLOPER HITLESS
AGAINST HAYMAKERS**

Slumping slugger costs Rounders the division lead. Now the pennant's as good as gone for our hometown has-beens!

Ouch! That smarted.

Really smarted.

Why would Gabby have written such a thing? I thought she liked me.

"We're not cold shouldering you, Walloper," explained Ocho from a couple seats away. "We just feel bad about what Gabby wrote in the paper. It's not your fault you forgot how to hit."

Ocho was trying to be nice, but his words only made me feel lousier. He was right. I had forgotten how to hit. Unless I remembered soon, the rotten newspaper would be right, too. The

Rounders would be as licked as lollipops. There was no way we'd ever catch the Haymakers if I didn't start hitting again.

And soon.

★ CHAPTER 9 ★

WE WHEELED INTO Lumleyville Park in a
swirling cloud of dust. Fans walking
across the parking lot to the field stopped and
stared at us as we piled out of the bus.

"Look! Look!" cried a kid in a white
Lumberjacks cap with a green pine-tree logo.
He was pointing right at me. "A rain cloud! A
huge rain cloud."

"Hooray!" The fans started cheering. "Rain
will end this miserable heat!"

Then the dust settled and the good people of
Lumleyville saw that I was not in fact a gathering storm. I was a baseball player mired in a
hitting slump.

People often got pretty charged up when the visiting team arrived to play their hometown heroes. Not these Lumberjacks fans, though. They just put down their heads and trudged toward the entrance gates. You would have thought they were on their way to summer school instead of a baseball game.

We went straight to the field to warm up.

In this weather, warming up was easy. You got warm just breathing. Fortunately, we weren't in any danger of overheating against the Lumberjacks. Those kids were born to cut trees. Taking cuts at the plate was another story. They knew how to saw lumber, but they didn't know how to swing it. They could chop wood all day, but they couldn't tell a chop grounder from chopped liver.

You get the point. Lumleyville dwelled in the cellar. We expected no trouble from those woodcutters.

We eased through our warm-ups, then gathered around Skip Lou in the dugout.

"It's hot and we've got a lot of innings to play," he said. "You guys make sure to drink plenty of water throughout the game. Other than that, business as usual. Except for one thing. I'm dropping Walloper a couple spots in the order. No big deal. Gasser will bat third, Tugboat moves up to the four spot."

My teammates all shot quick glances at me. I always batted third. Always. I smiled tightly and pretended the change didn't bother me at all.

"Just get on in front of me, guys," I said. "I'll break out the soap and clean up."

Everybody laughed.

Actually, I didn't like Skip's move one bit. It rattled me like a skeleton in a hurricane. Had he lost confidence in me so soon? After only one game? Did my slump really look that bad to him? If it did, then I was in even more trouble than I thought. Skip Lou had been around a long time. He was expert in all things baseball. Including slumps. Before I could dwell on it anymore, the game started.

"PLAY BALL!" barked the umpire.

I guess you could call what we played ball. But I don't know what game the Lumberjacks played. Tiddlywinks, maybe.

Against Mo Crandall, the soft-tossing Lumberjack starter, Stump, Ducks, and Gasser opened with back-to-back-to-back doubles. We had two runs on the board and one out when I came up, eager to show I could still wallop the ball. A doctor couldn't have prescribed a better cure for a slump than poor Mo Crandall. He threw about as hard as a bowl of mashed potatoes.

His first pitch to me hung in the air like a full moon. It was so beautiful I wanted to take a picture. Instead I swung. And I missed.

The next one was just as fat. I eased up a bit on the power, just trying to make contact. But the ball must have been feeling stuck-up. It didn't want to meet my bat at all. Strike two. All of a sudden, I got panicky. My mind started

racing. What if I struck out again? Would Skip bury me farther down in the lineup? Would the guys ever trust me again? While I was worrying about that stuff, Mo slipped a cream puff over the inside corner. Strike three. I was out of there.

In the bottom half of the inning, Slingshot set Lumleyville down, one-two-three. Out in the bleachers, ornery fans boiled like a pot of water. It was hard to tell whom they were madder at—us, the weather, or their own lousy, losing Lumberjacks. They hissed and booed every play. But their antics didn't slow us down one bit.

Gilly led off with a home run. No surprise there. After me, he was our best long-ball hitter. After the old me, that was. Next up was the eighth spot in the order, Octavio James. He was good enough to bat leadoff, but eight was his lucky number. It was also the source of his nickname, Ocho—Spanish for "eight." He followed Gasser's tater with one of his own. Next, the Glove scorched a base hit between short and third. Ducks followed with a sharp single, and Stump drew a walk on four pitches, loading the bases.

Normally I would've been up next, but now I watched from the bench as hard-swinging Gasser dug in at the plate. Oddly, I wasn't terribly upset over not batting. After the fiasco of my first-inning whiff, I was kind of glad. The thought of bombing again with the bases loaded weighed on my mind like the elephant in the old joke about the fence. You know, what time is it when an elephant sits on your fence? Time to get a new fence. Maybe it was time for the Rounders to get a new third baseman.

"Give it a ride now," I called weakly.

Swinging at the first pitch, Gasser jerked the bat around fast enough to make it dizzy. The ball whistled toward right field like a screech owl dive-bombing for mice. Leaping desperately, the first baseman somehow managed to snow cone the liner. He quickly stepped on the bag. Double play. I grabbed my mitt and headed out to third for the bottom half of the inning. I hoped the guys couldn't tell how relieved I was not to have batted. It was a chicken way to feel, but it was the truth.

The game moved along quickly. The Lumberjacks made outs; we made runs. We scored exactly twice in every inning and won the first game of the doubleheader by a score of 12–0.

Every Rounder knocked at least one hit.

Except me.

I went up four times, and four times I went down swinging.

My second oh-fer in two days.

Ouch. That smarted.

Really smarted.

★ CHAPTER 10 ★

BETWEEN GAMES, WE kicked back in the dugout and ate lunch. I took a seat next to Ocho and broke out my PB&Js. Mr. Bones sprawled at our feet. I tipped some water into the overturned Frisbee, and he lapped it up gratefully. From the relative cool of the concrete shelter, we watched Lumberjack fans file grimly out of the grandstand.

"Think they'll come back?" I asked Ocho.

"Sure," he said. "You can't abandon your team when it's down."

"I don't know," I said, chewing a bite of sandwich. "They didn't seem like such great fans to me. All that booing."

"Probably just this heat," he said generously. "It's enough to make anyone cranky."

Skip Lou wandered over and sat down beside us. "Good game, Ocho," he said. "You were dandy as candy out there." He turned to me. "How's your, uh, you know?" He asked, squinting at the ever-present cloud above my head.

"It's weird, Skip. That first pitch from Mo? I was sure I was going to clobber it. Then I swung right through it. I don't know; maybe the heat is getting to me. Next time, I'm thinking I'll crowd the plate. Then I'll shorten my swing and try to go the other way with it. Inside out, you know?"

"Listen, son," he said, "try not to think too much. Just go up there and do what you always do. Even Albert Pujols hits a dry patch now and then. Big leaguers will tell you the only thing to do is keep swinging. You'll get your groove back. It may take time, but it'll come."

He patted my shoulder and moved down the bench, offering praise and encouragement to all the Rounders.

I breathed a sigh of relief. At least Skip wasn't planning to totally bench me. Not yet, anyway. I didn't see how he could avoid it, though, if I didn't start hitting soon. We were in a pennant race. We needed production from every position. My mind began to race again. What if I really had forgotten how to hit? Images of failure ran through my head. A kid in the National Spelling Bee blanking on an easy word on prime-time TV. A kicker shanking a winning field goal in the final seconds of the Super Bowl. A snowboard racer falling over a phantom obstacle feet from the Olympic finish line. Me whiffing with two out in the bottom of the sixth in a one-run game.

"Walloper! Walloper!" Ocho hissed my name. He also dug me in the ribs with his elbow.

"Ouch!" I bleated, looking up. "What's the big idea?" Everybody was staring at me. I felt like I had missed something.

"It's her," Ocho whispered.

"Who?" I asked. Then I saw her. Gabby Hedron. Notebook in hand, camera around her neck, and trouble all over her face. My former friend skipped down the dugout steps.

She was the last person I wanted to see. After my dismal performance in the morning game, I could only imagine what her next story would say.

"Walloper strikes out so much he needs a new nickname. Great Walloper? More like the Great Whiffer."

"Hi guys," she said casually from the bottom

step. "Super game. Hey, Gasser, I noticed you moved up in the batting order. What was that like?"

"No comment," Gasser said coolly.

Gabby frowned slightly. "Okay," she said. "Free country. How about you, Tugboat? Think you guys can still catch the Haymakers?"

"Of course," the catcher replied.

"Care to elaborate?" Gabby asked.

"No."

"Look, guys," she muttered, avoiding eye contact with me. "I'm just trying to do my job. Won't any of you talk?"

My teammates weren't moved. They did their best impressions of broken clocks. They refused to give her the time of day.

"I guess I'll just have to write what I see," she said, shrugging her shoulders. "Good luck in the second game, guys. I'll be rooting for you. I always do."

With that, Gabby capped her pen. She did not look happy. Her face was flushed. Whether from heat or frustration, I did not know. Turning to leave the dugout, she nearly bumped into several parents who were coming down the steps. More specifically, she almost walked smack into my dad.

"Uh, hi, Mr. Bishbash," she mumbed. "Mrs. James. Mr. and Mrs. Phipps. Nice to see you. Some weather, huh?"

"Hello, Gabby," my dad said quietly. His face was half turned from me, and I couldn't see his expression. He sounded tired. I flashed back to breakfast, the way he'd tried to hide the paper so I wouldn't see Gabby's story. Poor Dad. I knew he must feel awkward bumping into her like that.

She must have felt uncomfortable too. We'd been friends for a long time. I felt a twinge of sadness for her as she walked away by herself. What she had said was true, I realized. She was only doing her job. If only I had been doing mine, namely hitting the ball, none of us would've been in this pickle.

Mrs. Phipps cleared the air by waving a couple boxes of ice-cream sandwiches in the air.

"You boys must be hot," she said brightly. "There are enough for everyone, if it's all right with Coach Clementine."

"Sure is, Marcy. As long as there's one with my name on it!"

Mrs. Phipps handed the boxes to Skip Lou. He tore off the tops and set them down on the end of the bench, triggering an ice-cream-sandwich stampede.

Dad stepped back from the melee and caught my eye.

"Good luck," he mouthed, flashing a thumbs-up. "I gotta get back to the office."

"Walloper," yelled Stump. "Think quick!"

He fired an ice-cream sandwich at me.

"Thanks!"

When I turned again to my dad, all I saw was his back as he left.

We were still licking chocolate off our fingers

when the second half of the doubleheader got under way.

"PLAY BALL!" the ump hollered.

The Lumberjacks picked right up where they had left off in the first game. They dropped pop-ups, booted grounders, and ran into each other like the diamond was a bumper-car track and they were the cars. We scored three runs off them in the top of the first.

As I took the field for the bottom of the inning, I noticed that Ocho had been right. The Lumberjack fans had come back. They had even brought friends with them. Lots of friends. The crowd looked like a carpenter's thumb after he hit it with a hammer. It was swollen. It was also sore. Every last person out there looked angry. And they all clutched brown paper bags.

"What do you s'pose they have in those sacks?" I shouted to Stump at short.

"Dunno," said Stump. "Cold sodas, maybe?"

"I don't think so," I said.

We didn't have to wait long to learn. As Slingshot fired his first pitch, the spectators crinkled open their bags and pulled out water balloons. They tried to pelt us, but the balloons had wilted in the heat. Misshapen and leaky, they wobbled through the air and landed harmlessly on the seared grass. The fans howled in despair. Nothing was going right for them. In the outfield, Ducks, Gasser, and Ocho took pity. They ran from their positions and stood close to the fences, where the irate fans could easily nail them. The guys hooted gleefully as a fresh barrage of water balloons broke over them.

"Aah," Gasser crowed when a fat blue one burst on his back. "That's nice. Do you have another? Don't be shy now."

After watching in amazement for a minute, our entire infield dropped our gloves and ran over to the sidelines, where we pleaded with the Lumleyville fans to pelt us. Soon, the Lumberjacks players stormed out of their dugout and got in on the action.

"Hit me, hit me!" players cried. "Please, please, please, throw one this way!"

The fans obliged. They darkened the sky with water balloons, and we did our best to get in the way of every single one. When we were all good and cool, we trotted back to our positions on the field, wet and happy as a bunch of river otters.

"PLAY BALL!" ordered the ump, scratching his head. I don't think he'd ever seen anything like it. I don't think anyone ever had.

By the third inning, we led the Lumberjacks 8–0, and balloon skins blanketed the brown grass of the outfield like a patchwork quilt.

In the fifth, Gasser tripled home a couple more runs. We ran our lead into double digits, and the ornery Lumberjack fans ran out of water balloons. Now they showered the field with torn-up scorecards. So much confetti fluttered through the air that it looked like a snowstorm.

A real snowstorm would have been nice. It would have cooled things down.

By the last inning, the Lumberjacks players looked like they wanted to get as far away as possible from Lumleyville Park. Three batters in a row swung wildly at every pitch they saw, gift wrapping a two-hitter for Slingshot. The final score was 14–0. Every Rounder had crushed at least three hits.

Except me.

My line was like a gopher without the g. It was another oh fer. Oh for five, to be exact. Five trips to the plate, five wimpy whiffs.

No doubt about it, my slump had reached epic proportions. On a scale of one to ten, it was an eleven. It was kryptonite. It was the *Titanic*. It was everything bad you could think of rolled into one and multiplied by two.

Despite it all, the Rounders had managed to win a pair of games. With only a few days left in the season, we still had a chance to catch the Haymakers.

But how far could we go if I didn't start con-
tributing?

That was the question.

I was afraid of the answer.

★ CHAPTER 11 ★

WHEN WE BOARDED THE team bus back to Rambletown, the old seats were hot from baking in the sun all day. Smoking hot. They were so fiery, you could have pitched camp around them and toasted marshmallows. It was like a regular bonfire on that bus.

Mr. Bones climbed up next to me in the back and that short-legged, long-nosed, yellow-haired fur ball just lay there panting. He was too done in by the heat to even bother licking my face. This was not like him at all. He was a dog who liked to be petted and liked to lick faces.

We opened all the windows to let in a

breeze, but the only thing that wafted into the bus was hot, sticky air. Hot air and some balloon skins. Boy, the heat was really starting to wear on me. Between the weather, the doubleheader, and my hitting woes, I was feeling pretty done in.

Tugboat flipped on his radio. He fiddled with the dial and tuned in WHOT 102.5. Soon we

heard DJ Louie "the Lip" Leibenstraub giving a weather report.

The Lip said:

"THE RECORD HEAT IS THE HOTTEST ON RECORD. IT'S GOING TO STAY HOT, HOT, HOT AND HAZY, HAZY, HAZY, WITH NO RELIEF IN SIGHT."

We all groaned.

"BUT HOT IS HOW WE LIKE IT OVER HERE AT HOT 102.5, THE HOTTEST STATION ON THE PLANET. IN HONOR OF THE HEAT WAVE, LET'S GO TO THE VAULT FOR SOME CLASSIC ROCK BY BLUE ÖYSTER CULT. HERE'S "BURNIN' FOR YOU" FROM ALL THE WAY BACK IN THE STEAMY SUMMER OF 1981."

As the song kicked on and the sound of crashing guitars filled the bus, we all groaned again.

"Nineteen eighty-one!" cried Stump. "Did

they even *have* music back then?"

"Caveman music," hooted the Glove, "like from the Dark Ages. This racket is horrible."

"We should call the Lip and make a request," suggested Gasser. "Like something by Cheese Sprocket. They rock!"

Tugboat grinned and turned up the volume. "My parents love this station," he said.

"I'm burning, I'm burning, I'm burning for you," crooned the slick-voiced singer. *"I'm burning, I'm burning, I'm burning for you!"*

"Somebody get that man a fire extinguisher," yelled Stump, cracking us up.

Our laughter drowned out the music. Tugboat cranked up the volume, but the song had ended, replaced by an ad for Dolphin Dan's Water World.

"Dolphin Dan's!" shouted Gilly. "That place is awesome! You guys ever been? They've got this gigantic waterslide shaped like a volcano. It must be twenty stories tall. Remember, Billy?"

Billy nodded. The look on his face, half

smile, half grimace, suggested that maybe he had mixed feelings about the towering waterslide. "There's a coral reef, too." He gulped. "That's cool. Sometimes you can find stuff in the rocks."

"We should go," Gilly continued, bouncing out of his seat. "We should all go right after practice tomorrow. Team trip! Who's up for it?"

A brilliant plan was quickly hatched to recruit our parents to bring us to Dolphin Dan's Water World. Who could turn down a day at a water park in the middle of a heat wave? Slapping high fives, we congratulated ourselves on our cleverness. Dolphin Dan's, here we come. We were going to have a blast.

In the excitement, everybody forgot about the pennant and the Haymakers and my slump. For a moment, they did. Then Kid Rabbit Winkle happened to glance my way. I could tell by his widening eyes that my big nasty had gotten bigger and nastier. One by one, the Rounders followed his gaze. Suddenly, things got awfully quiet on the bus. For the rest of the way home, nobody mentioned Dolphin Dan's. Nobody said much of anything at all.

By the time we pulled into Rambletown, my slump pretty much filled the bus. Ducking low to avoid it, my teammates slunk away in a hurry. Nobody wanted to catch what I had.

As I trudged down the steps, Skip Lou swiveled in the driver's seat and took me by the arm.

"Get some rest," he muttered, avoiding my eyes. "Maybe it'll clear up by morning." Then he closed the door, leaving me and Mr. Bones alone on the sidewalk. As we made our way home through the sticky afternoon, our only company was my slump. It hung over my head like a black umbrella as I walked. A real umbrella would have been nice. It would have provided some shade.

Mom and Dad didn't have to say "just ten more minutes" that night. They didn't have to threaten to unplug the ZBox, or yell for me to stop fielding bouncers off the side of the garage and come inside, like they sometimes do. They didn't have to remind me to brush my teeth or take off my socks or any of that stuff. After a quick dinner, I went straight up to my room and got ready for bed without any prodding. That's how tired I was. Tired from playing a double-header, tired of the oppressive heat, and, most of all, tired of my slump.

I put on my pj's and carefully hung my Rounders uniform on the hook on the back of the closet door. It occurred to me that maybe I should hang it up for good. It was a sick, sad thought, but it was one I had to face. If I couldn't hit, what was the sense in playing baseball?

Like he always did, Mr. Bones followed me into my room. But for the first time in his life, that short-legged, long-nosed, yellow-haired fur ball did not jump up on the bed with me. He turned three sad little circles and curled up like a pill bug on the floor in the corner.

"You too, Mr. Bones?" I said.

★ CHAPTER 12 ★

IN THE MORNING, THINGS were not better. They were worse. What made them worse was the *Rambletown Bulletin.*

Gabby's article said:

Walloper has become a human playground. He's full of swings that don't go anywhere. His slump is so deep, a scuba diver could dive in and never reach the bottom.

I tried to digest the story over a bowl of Pirate Crunch. The cereal didn't go down much easier than Gabby's words. Those frosted marshmallow cannonballs looked more like baseballs than ever. Slippery little baseballs that kept sliding off my spoon as I tried to get ahold of them.

What did she have against me? I wondered. Racking my brain for an answer, I recalled the last conversation I'd had with her. We'd talked the morning my picture appeared in the paper, right before our game against the Haymakers. The morning my slump started. It was only a couple days earlier, but it secmed like a million years. Everything was so great back then. I was still hitting. The Rounders still had a chance to beat the Haymakers. Gabby had been so confident, she had crowed in the paper that'd I'd probably wallop a home run off Flicker Pringle.

That's when it hit me. After talking to Gabby that morning, I had run out on the field. Stump had started needling me, and I'd told him

Gabby didn't know what she was talking about. Had she heard me? That would be awful. I hadn't meant it. Gabby was great. She was my friend.

At least, she had been. I was just miffed that she had predicted I would hit a homer off Flicker Pringle. Making predictions was asking for bad luck. Plus, I wanted Stump to stop needling me. That was the only reason I'd said that.

Now I felt worse than ever. It was one thing to strike out in a baseball game. It was another to hurt someone's feelings. It was far worse.

Gabby and I needed to talk.

Just then, the doorbell rang. Mr. Bones raced over to the door, tail swishing like a windshield wiper set on high. That's one thing about him: you can't keep him down for long. He may have been dejected the night before, but the sight of Stump and Slingshot standing on the porch perked him right up. It didn't do much for my mood though.

"Why are you still in your pj's?" Stump asked

as I let them in. He and Slingshot wore back-packs. "We've got practice in ten minutes."

"Skip Lou will make us run laps if we're late." Slingshot groaned. "It's way too hot to run laps."

"You guys go without me," I said glumly.

"But you'll miss Dolphin Dan's!" Stump exclaimed. "It's all set. Ocho's and Gilly's moms are driving."

I really wanted to go, but what was the point? The guys would have more fun without me and my bloated blimp of a slump tagging along. One look at that thing would ruin every-body's day. Besides, I should really find Gabby and apologize.

"I don't know." I shrugged.

"Get it together, Walloper!" Stump shouted. "You've got to come. Right, Slingshot?"

"Team trip means the whole team goes," Slingshot said. "If you bag, we all bag. That's the way it works with teams. Personally, I would never forgive you. I've never been to

Dolphin Dan's, and I'm really looking forward to it."

"You want me to come? Seriously?"

"All for one and one for all," said Slingshot. "Besides, maybe you can drown that thing at the water park." He eyed my slump.

"Not funny!" I shouted.

"Walloper, will you please just get dressed?" Stump pleaded. "Throw a pair of swim trunks and a towel into your backpack. We're leaving straight from practice. You asked your parents, right?"

"Asked what?" questioned my mom, coming into the kitchen.

I explained about Dolphin Dan's.

"Sounds like a good way to stay cool to me," Mom said.

"Thanks, Mom!" I raced upstairs.

Two minutes later, Slingshot, Stump, and I rattled out the door. Mr. Bones stayed home. Dogs were not allowed at Dolphin Dan's. It was unfair. Mr. Bones loved to swim.

Racing through air as thick as motor oil, we made it to the park in record time. Good thing, too. If we hadn't hustled, we would have been ten minutes late, rather than only five. The extra five minutes would have meant one more punishment lap.

"Glad you fellows could grace us with your presence," Skip Lou said as we huffed onto the field, red faced as lobsters. "Now get going." He drew a circle in the humid air to show that he expected us to lap the field. Rules were rules.

Slingshot and Stump shot me dirty looks as we set off down the first baseline. I felt terrible. Slingshot was right. It was too hot to run. But because of me, we had no choice. We'd dashed all the way to the park and now we had to keep going. Man, I was nothing but a big, fat curse to my teammates.

"Welcome back," Skip Lou teased when we finished our circuit of the field. He filled cups of water for us from the cooler. "Now that we're all here, how about a round of bull's-eye?"

The guys nodded eagerly. Bull's-eye was everyone's favorite drill.

"Just the thing to get us hitting again," Skip said. He graciously did not mention me by name.

The way the game worked, we split into two teams. Both sides took turns trying to smack easy pitches into mesh batting-practice screens set up around the diamond, one on the left side, one on the right side, and one in front of the mound. Every time you nailed a screen, you scored a point for your team. The key was choking up on the bat and not swinging too hard. In bull's-eye, you didn't try to kill the ball. It was all about making contact. If your mechanics were good, the screens were sitting ducks. Whichever squad hit the most targets won. The prize was watching the other guys run around the field.

The Losers' Lap, we called it.

I took the field with Slingshot, Gilly, the Glove, and Kid Rabbit. We were the Reds. Right-handed Ocho batted first for the Blues.

"Left side," he shouted as Skip soft-tossed

the first of four pitches to him. Ocho hit the ball solidly, sending it into the net on two bounces. On his next try, he swung a shade late and rolled the ball foul. The two after that he peppered straight back to the middle screen.

"Excellent bat control," Skip Lou praised. "Three points. Who's next?"

Gasser took a couple practice cuts and then squared up. A lefty, he ripped the first pitch wide of the target between first and second. Gilly retrieved the ball and threw it back to Skip. Gasser jumped all over the next one, drilling the ball so hard up the middle that it nearly tore a hole in the screen.

"Easy, tiger." Skip laughed. "I'm just the designated pitcher."

Gasser grinned sheepishly, then narrowly missed depositing a couple winners in the left-side target. Ducks replaced him at the plate and managed two out of four. Stump did the same. Then it was Tugboat's turn. Choking up like Ichiro, the quick-handed catcher sprayed hits left, center, right, and left again for four points. That gave the Blues twelve.

"Hot stuff!" Skip shouted. "Now let's see what the Reds can do."

Slingshot went first. Calling his shots like a pool shark, he buried four out of four. Next up, Gilly poked two pitches into the right target, giving us six points. The third missed the middle target by the thickness of an earthworm. A skinny earthworm, at that. The last one he blasted into center field.

"Where were you going with that?" Skip asked as Ocho chased down the long fly. "Canada?"

Gilly shrugged, abashed, and handed the bat to the Glove. The speedy second baseman whistled Skip's first pitch into the left screen. He bounced over the middle target on his second try, then drilled two into the right screen for a couple more points. 12–9, Blues. Kid Rabbit took over from there and alternated solid hits with a couple of near misses. We were up to eleven, one behind the Blues.

"Way to get after it." Skip applauded. "You're one run down with one hitter to go. Ready, Walloper?"

I nodded. "Stay calm," I told myself. "Nice, easy swings."

Nice and easy sure described Skip's first pitch. He hung it over the plate like a baseball-shaped piñata.

"Right side!" I called.

My swing followed through to the right side, but the ball didn't go anywhere except past me. It landed behind home plate and rolled to the backstop.

"Shake it off, kid," Slingshot called. "One to tie! That's all you need!"

When I missed the next one, and the one after that, Skip shook his head. I couldn't tell if he was angry or sad. I choked up for pitch number four, my last chance to tie the score.

"C'mon, Walloper, clock it now," my Red teammates urged desperately. Immediately, the Blues picked up the cry. They may have wanted to win at bull's-eye, but more than that, they wanted to see me hit the ball again. For the team's sake and mine, I needed to lay some wood on cowhide.

The ball floated toward me as gentle as a dove. I lunged at it. I missed. The cheering died as quickly as it had started.

"Good job, Blue team," Skip said, looking mystified. "See you later, Reds."

For the third time that morning, Stump and Slingshot had to get the lead out because of me. All this running around would've been great if we were training for the Boston Marathon or something. But we weren't. We were trying to win a pennant. We set off with Gilly and Kid Rabbit on the Losers' Lap, jogging slowly around the sun-baked field. Our heavy footfalls made the only sounds. Dust puffed up from the dry earth at every step. We were all too embarrassed to speak.

At least I was too embarrassed.

For all I knew, the guys were probably too angry.

★ CHAPTER 13 ★

A MATCHING PAIR OF blue minivans waited to take us to Dolphin Dan's Water World.

"Which one's yours?" Slingshot asked Gilly as we finished our lap.

Before he could answer, the side door of the van closest to us slid open and little Billy Wishes's yellow head popped out.

"Let's roll!" he called.

We piled in, filling the middle and back rows. I slumped into the seat and tried to forget my awful showing at bull's-eye. Mrs. Wishes had the AC cranking full blast, and the chilled air washed over me like an ocean wave. It felt so good, I could've been happy sitting there all day. Who needed a water park when you had a giant refrigerator on wheels?

"Seat belts on, everybody?" Mrs. Wishes called over her shoulder. "Okay, Dolphin Dan's, here we come!"

She tootled the horn and we convoyed out of the lot. Our route to the highway took us through downtown Rambletown, past the library and City Hall, everything eerily deserted in the midday heat. It was as if the whole town had been abducted by aliens.

We picked up the highway and had been barreling along for a few minutes when Billy let out a whoop from his window seat.

"There it is!" he exclaimed.

Looking where he pointed, I saw the huge man-made volcano of Dolphin Dan's looming above the trees in the distance. The thing looked so real it was kind of scary, all craggy and bumpy and topped with a jagged crater. Fiery orange sluices streaked down the steep sides like flowing lava.

"Faster, Mom!" Gilly pleaded.

When the vans zipped into the lot a few minutes later, I saw where everyone in Rambletown had disappeared to. People hadn't been abducted by aliens after all. They'd all come to Dolphin Dan's. The place was like a suitcase at the airport. Packed.

We paid at the gate and hustled past a pair of dolphin statues into a tropical-looking picnic grove. Grabbing an open table, the moms called us together to lay down the rules.

"Listen up, gang," Mrs. James said. "I want everybody to pick a buddy and stick to him like glue. If you get separated, come find Claire and me right here. Let's all meet up here at twelve thirty for lunch. It's not quite eleven now, so that gives you a little more than an hour and a half."

Mrs. Wishes nodded, adding, "Gilly, you look out for Billy."

With that, we raced off to the changing rooms to slip into our swimming trunks. As we stuffed our street clothes into lockers, I overheard a man sitting at the end of the bench talking into a cell phone.

"I can't find my watch anywhere," he said sadly. "Maybe it came off on the slide, but I looked and didn't see it."

Hearing that, I checked my own wrist to make sure my own watch was buckled tightly. Then Tugboat led the charge out to the volcano.

"To the summit, men!" He hollered, and we followed him to the chairlift that would carry us to the top.

The dangling chairs swept us up the volcano. Far below, sliders rocketed down winding, lava-colored water chutes and plunged into a tropical lagoon. The closer we got to the top, the louder their screams rang out and the harder our hearts pounded. Reaching the summit, we jumped off the chairlift and joined a line. The line moved quickly. One person after another disappeared down the steep chute, leaving behind only ring-ing screams. Far below, in the grove, Gilly's and Ocho's moms waved at us from the picnic table.

They were like two little specks. We waved back. It felt kind of silly waving to specks.

"It's really high," Billy said anxiously.

"You'll be fine," Gilly reassured him. "I'll be right behind you the whole way."

"And I'll be right in front," chimed in Gasser.

"And I'll be right in front of him," said Ducks.

"And I'll be right in front of him," said the Glove.

We kept at it until everybody had listed who'd they be in front of or behind. "And when we get to the bottom," we told Billy, "we'll all turn around and wait for you."

"It'll be fun," Gilly assured his little brother.

Then we were at the head of the line and it was go time. Tugboat shoved off first, shouting "Geronimo" as he slipped over the edge. We tumbled after him like dominoes. Or lemmings, those funny little hamsterlike critters that supposedly line up to jump off cliffs in Norway. Ocho, Slingshot, the Glove, Ducks, Gasser,

Billy, Gilly, Stump, Kid Rabbit, and me, in that order. I wondered if it was just coincidence that I was buried at the bottom of the order.

When I got to the front, I didn't think I would make it. It wasn't the dizzying height that bothered me. It was my low-flying slump. For a minute it looked like there was no way it would fit under the grab bar. The teenage attendant stared at me like I had two heads.

"Holy cow, kid, what is that thing?" he asked.

"It's my slump," I mumbled.

"It looks like a parachute," he exclaimed. "Won't it slow you down?"

"It already has," I said sadly. "On the baseball diamond."

Finally, I squeezed under the bar and found myself hurtling down the slide on a rushing current of ice-cold water. The water felt great. For the first time since the heat wave had started, I didn't feel like I was roasting alive. As I whipped through the curves, I remembered Slingshot's crack about drowning my

slump. Figuring it was worth a shot, I dipped my head back into the fast-moving water. It was like bobbing for apples. Only backward. Suddenly, the track ended and I was launched through the air into the lagoon. The cold water closed deliciously over me.

A second later, I popped to the surface to the cheers and laughter of the guys. First thing I did was check for my slump. The bad news was that it was still in place. The good news was, I didn't care. I was having too much fun to worry about it.

"That," I said, water streaming down my face, "was awesome."

"You should have seen Billy," Gilly said proudly. "He flew off that jump like he had wings!"

Billy smiled and said he might try again later. For the moment he wanted to explore the fake coral reef on the other side of the lagoon. Gilly went off with him, and the rest of us headed back up the volcano.

The second ride was as good as the first. Maybe even better, because this time down I wasn't worried about surviving the splash landing. The ride passed in a blur, and soon I found myself slicing once more into the lagoon.

The cool water covered me like a thick liquid blanket. When I surfaced, I saw the guys gathered at the edge of the sandy white beach. Mrs. Wishes and Ocho's mom were there too, talking to another grown-up. Gilly waved me over.

"Billy found a watch," he said excitedly as I waded onto the beach. "An expensive one, like scuba divers wear. It was stuck in a crack in the coral. Still working and everything."

Blinking water out of my eyes, I recognized the man on the beach as the guy I'd seen in the changing room. He was shaking Billy's hand and thanking him.

"It was a birthday present from my wife," he said. "I was afraid I'd lost it forever. I'd like to give you a reward. How about an ice cream?"

Billy looked at his mom. She nodded.

"Sure," Billy said.

The man with the watch noticed the rest of us looking at him.

"Oh, why not?" he said. "Cones for all your friends, too."

We roared happily. Billy ruled! He was the luckiest kid ever. Later, on the way home, I made sure to sit next to him in the minivan. Maybe some of his good fortune would rub off on me.

★ CHAPTER 14 ★

WE DIDN'T HAVE PRACTICE the next day. At least, the Rounders didn't have practice. I sure did. First thing in the morning, I got my old batting tee out of the garage and set it up in the backyard.

"Baby steps," I told Mr. Bones, who bounded eagerly at my side.

I placed a rubber ball on the tee and took a couple cuts with one of my old bats. The bat felt fine and balanced in my hands.

"You've got to walk before you can run," I said. Mr. Bones wagged his tail. "And you've got to crawl before you can walk." I stepped up to the tee and took careful aim. I hadn't hit a ball off a tee since kindergarten. I swung. I hit the ball. It soared across the yard. I felt like I had just won the World Series with a walk-off salami.

"Take that, slump!" I hollered.

Mr. Bones raced after the ball and brought it back to me. I placed it on top of the tee and took another whack. Line drive into the shrubs at the edge of the yard.

"Go get it, boy!" I said. Mr. Bones disappeared into the bushes, popping out a minute later with the ball in his mouth.

We kept at it for a solid hour, working up a lather in the steamy heat. My slump still hung over my head as big as ever, but at least I was making solid contact on every swing. Apparently, the slump only affected me when the ball was pitched. This was puzzling, but I took it as a good sign. There didn't seem to be anything fundamentally wrong with my swing.

Mr. Bones and I would have kept at it longer, except Stump and Slingshot showed up on their bikes. I heard them before I saw them. A battery-powered bike radio was fastened to Stump's frame, and it was blaring an oldie called "Heat Wave" as my friends cruised into the yard. They pulled up and watched me spank a few balls across the lawn.

"Progress?" Slingshot asked.

"I think so," I said, knocking one into a towering old oak tree.

"Looking good," said Stump. "Think you can do it off a live pitcher?"

"We'll find out soon enough," I said. "Man, it's hot."

"Sticky as chewing gum," said Slingshot. He blew a bubble until it popped.

I dropped the bat and we plopped into plastic lawn chairs in the shade. My mom came out with a pitcher of lemonade and three glasses.

"Jeter or Jimmy Rollins?" Stump asked after

we'd had a drink. Major League shortstops were his favorite subject.

"Definitely Jeter," said Slingshot. "He does it all. Hits for average, drives in runs, and steals bases. Plus, he's got rings. Four of them."

"Rollins puts up monster numbers and he's won an MVP," I argued. "He had something like 30 homers, 40 steals, and 90 runs batted in for the Phillies in his MVP year. Sick stats for a shortstop. Jeter can't touch that."

"Actually, their career slugging averages are pretty close," said Stump. "Jeter's is four sixty, Rollins's comes out to four forty-one. They both average a hair better than 16 home runs a season. Of course, Jeter has been playing longer, 14 seasons to 9 for Rollins, so the Yankee captain's career totals are higher. He's got more than 200 homers, while Rollins should soon break 150. Also, they both score a boatload of runs—over a hundred every season."

"What are you, some kind of walking baseball encyclopedia?" Slingshot asked. "How do you remember all those numbers?"

Stump's knowledge of stats and trivia had always amazed us.

"I'm a shortstop," Stump scoffed. "I have to know what I'm up against."

The song on the radio ended and the DJ Louie the Lip came on with the weather report.

"THE RECORD HEAT IS HOT, HOT, HOT AND THE HUMIDITY IS HIGH, HIGH, HIGH," HE SAID. "THE ONLY THING TO DO IS DRINK PLENTY OF FLUIDS AND KEEP YOUR RADIO TUNED TO HOT 102.5, THE HOTTEST STATION ON THE PLANET."

We didn't need the Lip to tell us it was hot. We could feel it.

Stump went over to his bike and fiddled with the radio dial. After some static, he picked up a ball game.

"IT'S A HOT DAY FOR BASEBALL, AND TWO OF

*THE HOTTEST TEAMS IN THE LEAGUE ARE
SET TO SQUARE OFF. THE ST. JOE JUNGLE
CATS HAVE TAKEN THE FIELD AND WILL BAT
LAST AGAINST THE VISITING HOG CITY
HAYMAKERS."*

The Jungle Cats were a pretty good team
with a plenty bad name. The Rounders had
played over in St. Joe many times, and I knew
for a fact there were no jungles within a hundred miles. The only cats I had ever seen were
regular old house cats.

"Grant Vesper is on the mound for the Cats,"
the announcer announced. "Here's the windup
and the pitch. Strike one to Haymaker lead-off
man, Rube Nardley."

"Way to go, Grant," cheered Slingshot.

We refilled our glasses and sat back to listen. Grant struck out Rube and retired the next
two guys on grounders. In the bottom of the
inning, Flicker Pringle set down the Jungle
Cats in order.

"Looks like Flicker Pringle brought his A game today," the announcer said. "His pitches are popping, let me tell you. We go to the second with no score."

We all groaned. If the Jungle Cats could somehow manage to win, we would still have a chance at the pennant. But nobody beat Flicker Pringle when he had his best stuff. It was like spitting into the wind. You just didn't do it.

Hanky Burns led off the second with a single for the Haymakers, but the Jungle Cats doubled him up on a comebacker to Grant. The pitcher then struck out the next batter, for out number three. In the bottom half, Flicker fanned the side.

"After two, there's still no score," said the announcer.

The Haymakers made no hay at the plate in the third. Instead, they made three straight outs. Our ears perked up a little bit. This was getting interesting. The Haymakers should've been steamrolling the Jungle Cats. St. Joe was decent, but they weren't nearly as good as the reigning champs.

"We ought to see this in person," Slingshot said.

He was right. Our pennant dreams hung on the outcome of the game. We needed to get over there and root our hearts out for the home team.

"We can make it in ten minutes," Stump pointed out.

"What are we waiting for?" I asked.

I ran inside to tell my folks where we were going, then we jumped on our bikes. The three of us pedaled hard for St. Joe, Mr. Bones running along beside us.

★ CHAPTER 15 ★

WE ARRIVED AT THE park at the end of the fourth inning and found seats close to the field on the third-base side. Mr. Bones crawled into the shade under the wooden bench. A quick check of the scoreboard showed nothing but zeros. Neither team had scored yet.

They didn't score in the fifth, either. The game went to the sixth, and final, inning still knotted at nothing.

This was getting really interesting. And tense. Stump, Slingshot, and I perched on the edges of our seats.

"Down in front," hollered someone sitting a row behind us. "You there, you're blocking my view!"

Did he mean us?

Slowly, I craned around. Sure enough, a red-faced man was pointing right at me. More precisely, he was pointing at my big, fat slump.

"What were you thinking, bringing that . . . that monstrosity . . . to the game?" he shouted. "I can't see the field. Keep it down, can't you?"

I *am* down, I thought, slumping low in my seat. I'm about as down as a person can possibly get. I felt like joining Mr. Bones under the bleachers.

Maybe I should have.

"I still can't see!" bellowed the angry man.

"This is getting embarrassing," mumbled Stump. "Can't you do anything?"

"Do you think I like lugging this thing around?" I snapped.

Humiliated, I slunk out of the row and up the steps. I watched the rest of the game standing against the wall at the very top row of the covered grandstand. It was a lousy vantage point, but the game was so good I was still glad I'd come.

To open the sixth, the Haymakers drew a walk off Grant Vesper. My heart sank a little. The next batter struck out and my heart rose up again. But then the runner took second on a fielder's choice. So it was two down with the go-ahead run on second when that mean old humdinger Flicker Pringle came up to bat. Our hearts dropped lower than a sinker pitch. Everybody knew that Flicker could hit the ball even harder than he could throw it.

Sure enough, he smacked the first pitch he saw straight toward the bleachers.

The ball soared high and deep. The Jungle Cat center fielder turned and ran after it. He kept right on chasing it until he ran out of real estate. At the wall, he turned and jumped like a jackalope. The ball fell toward the seats. Our hearts dropped like sandbags. As good as Flicker Pringle was on the mound, a two-run homer would all but ice the game. Real ice would

have been nice. It would've been cold.

The center fielder reached out with his glove until his whole arm was over the wall. Then he crashed back to earth, landing on his butt on the warning track. For a second he just lay there. Slowly, he raised his glove hand. Peeking over the webbing was the baseball.

He had stolen a tater from Flicker Pringle! It was the greatest catch I had ever seen.

In the grandstand, we all went bonkers. I jumped so high my slump bounced off the ceiling.

The game went to the bottom of the sixth, knotted at zero.

As the teams changed sides, I saw Slingshot pull out his cell phone and punch in a number.

"Who can you possibly be calling at a time like this?" I cried down to him.

Slingshot turned my way. "My guardian angel," he said. "We can use all the help we can get." He laughed, adding, "Just kidding—it's Gilly. He's got to know what's happening here."

As Slingshot gave Gilly the rundown, Flicker Pringle stomped out to the mound and kicked the dirt like a bull. Getting robbed of that home run had made him mad. He pounded his mitt so hard with his fist that it sounded like thunder. Real thunder would have been nice. It would have meant rain was coming.

The Jungle Cat batter dug in at the plate. Flicker Pringle stared him down. His eyes were hot and smoky, the way they got when he was really worked up. He kicked and delivered. Fastball right down the middle for strike one. Working quickly, Flicker delivered a hard one. Strike two on the outside corner. He wound up and fired another laser.

Whoosh went the swing.

"Yowch!" cried the backup's backup catcher.

"STEE-RIKE THREE!" roared the ump all too familiarly.

Flicker whiffed the next batter on three straight fastballs. That made two outs. With the inning slipping away, the crowd got quieter than a guitar with no strings.

In the sudden hush, Slingshot's voice rang clear. "Uh-oh," he said into his phone. "Not looking so good, Gilly. The Cats are down to one out now."

Flinging marbles, Flicker blew two quick strikes past the batter.

The poor kid from St. Joe stood in the batter's box, his legs quivering like a bowl of Jell-O doing a hula dance. In the bleachers, we started to think about next season. With Flicker throwing pure butane, the kid was toast. He wouldn't get a hit. The Jungle Cats wouldn't win the game, and we wouldn't catch the Haymakers in the standings. Flicker kicked for the heavens and fired a moonbeam.

That was when things got crazy.

The batter didn't even think about swinging. He just tossed his stick and hit the dirt like he was leaping out of the way of a runaway truck. I'd never seen anything like it. Fast as that pitch was coming, it was hard to blame him.

Game over, I thought. Season over.

But the fat lady hadn't quite taken the stage. She was warming up her vocal chords, but she wasn't singing yet.

Flicker's pitch collided with the bat in midair, shattering it into tiny pieces. The next thing I knew, the ump was signaling fair ball.

With the Haymaker catcher scrabbling around on his hands and knees, the runner took off for first. The ball was buried under shards of the splintered bat. The runner crossed the bag and made the big turn toward second. The catcher still couldn't find the ball, so the entire Haymaker infield rushed in to help look. Seeing the bases unguarded, the runner didn't slow down. He tagged second and headed for third.

In the excitement, I forgot about my slump and joined the fans streaming toward the field. We all wanted to get close to see what was going to happen.

I caught up with Slingshot and Stump in the

front row. We leaned over the rail, cheering like mad for the runner.

"He's rounding third and gunning for home!" Slingshot screamed into his phone.

"Go! Go! Go!" we chanted as he chugged down the line.

He was ten feet from home when Flicker reached into a wad of sawdust and pulled out the ball.

"Flicker Pringle has the ball!" Slingshot shouted to Gilly. "He stuck his hand in like Little Jack Horner and pulled out the ball like it was a plum."

The runner slid.

Flicker dived.

It was going to be close.

Dust and wood chips filled the air. We couldn't see the plate.

"It's as dark as a can of black paint on a moonless night down there," Slingshot said into his phone.

Stump and I didn't say anything to anyone.

We were holding our breath.

"SAFE!" cried the umpire, loud and clear.

A roar that sounded like a thousand jet airplanes rose from the stands. The St. Joe Jungle Cats had beaten the mighty Hog City Haymakers. They had won the game on the first dropped-bat-bunt-inside-the-park-infield-home run in the history of baseball.

Slingshot, Stump, and I leaped into the air like Olympic high jumpers. We high-fived each other and perfect strangers until our hands went numb.

"What?! What happened?!" Gilly's muffled voice buzzed from the phone. Slingshot had forgotten he was still on the line.

"The Jungle Cats won!" Slingshot screamed. "The Jungle Cats won and we're still alive. We can still take the pennant!"

It was true. We still could.

If only I started hitting again.

★ CHAPTER 16 ★

RIDING BACK FROM St. Joe under the cloud of my slump, the excitement of the Jungle Cats insane win began to wear off. What good did it do us, I wondered, with this slump dogging me? Flicker Pringle could spot me an *H* and an *I*, and I still wouldn't be able to make a hit out of it. And Hit was my middle name. Banjo Hit Bishbash. All I could think was how awful it would be to cost the Rounders the pennant with yet another whiff.

I could just imagine Gabby's caption in the *Rambletown Bulletin*:

Ramblers lose the pennant on Walloper's game-ending strikeout. One-time hero is like a piece of driftwood. He's all washed up!

I still hadn't talked to her. I really needed to do that.

When we reached our street, Stump and Slingshot peeled off for their houses. I pedaled the rest of the way home with Mr. Bones. Mom was toasting bread and frying baloney when we came through the door. But I couldn't even think about eating. My stomach was an old tree. It was full of knots.

"Oh, Banjie," Mom said. "You've got to eat."

Just as I was shaking my head, Dad burst in from work. He was all excited. The subject quickly changed from food to baseball.

"What a game!" Dad exclaimed. "I listened on the radio!"

"Yup," I said glumly.

"The first dropped-bat-bunt-inside-the-park-infield home run in the history of baseball! Wow! Who could've guessed it? If you read it in a book, you'd never believe it. Not in a million years!"

"Yup," I repeated.

"I'll bet old Flicker Pringle isn't feeling so big and tough right now!"

Yup," I said again. What I thought was, He's got to be more steamed up than a hot tub after losing that one. Pity the fools who face him next. He'll be out for blood. Oh, yeah, we face him next.

"You have those horrible Haymakers just where you want them!" Dad exclaimed. He was so excited he practically tap danced across the kitchen. "I know you can beat them!"

"That's right!" said Mom. "I can't wait! We'll be there with bells on, just as late as ever! You can count on that!"

"Yup," I said again.

I didn't have the heart to tell them what I was really thinking. Which was: How in the world do you expect us to beat the Haymakers with this slump hanging over me? I should just stay home. The only thing I can bring the guys is bad luck.

Bad luck and strikeouts.

Instead, I just sighed and said yup one more time.

In bed that night, I felt like I tossed and turned forever. But I guess I fell asleep at some point, because I was in la-la land when something rattled loudly against my window. I sat up with a start. The window rattled again. Louder this time.  It sounded like an apatosaurus-sized june bug was trying to flap his way into the room.

Mr. Bones sprang to the window and put his paws up on the sill. I slipped out of bed and padded over after him to see what was going on. I opened the window and poked out my head. The warm night air wrapped itself around me.

"Psst!" rose a voice from the grass below. "Hey, Walloper! Wake up! Are you awake, Walloper?"

"I am now," I said, rubbing my eyes. It was

pitch-black outside. I couldn't see a thing. "Who's there?"

"It's me, Stump," said the voice.

"And me," chimed in another voice. "Slingshot."

"Me too," piped up Ducks.

"Don't forget about me," added Gasser.

One by one, my teammates identified themselves. All of the Rounders were down there. In my front yard. In the middle of the night.

"What are you guys doing?" I whispered. "Don't you know we have a big game tomorrow?"

"That's why we're here," whispered Stump. His whisper was loud enough to quiet a thunderstorm. A real thunderstorm would have been nice. It would have cooled things down.

"On account of the game?" I asked. "I don't get it." Maybe I was still half asleep or something. I didn't have a clue what they were talking about.

"On account of the slump," corrected Stump.

"We're going to get rid of it. We've got a plan."

"A plan?" I said.

I looked at the clock glowing on my bureau. It read 11:48. Not quite midnight. I'd never been awake that late.

"How are you going to get rid of my slump?" I asked, suspicious.

"Leave that to us," Slingshot called back. "Just get down here. We'll meet you by the oak tree. Now!"

Well, sneaking out of the house at almost midnight was strange. But then again, so was my slump. If my friends knew how to make it go away, I was ready to listen. Nothing had worked so far. Not batting practice, not bull's-eye, not T-ball, not even fried-baloney sandwiches. What did I have to lose? I'd already lost my ability to hit. And the team had already lost one game to the Haymakers because of it. We sure couldn't afford to lose another.

I pulled on a pair of shorts and a T-shirt over my pj's, laced up my sneakers, and tiptoed toward the door. They were my shortie Batman pj's, and I kind of didn't want the guys to see me in them. Then I had a thought.

I tiptoed back to the window.

"Hey, guys," I whisper-called. "Should I bring my bat?"

"Forget the bat," cried Billy. "Just get a move on! We've got to do this at midnight. That's the witching hour."

The batboy's voice trailed away as he darted around the house toward the big oak tree in back. With Mr. Bones by my side, I slipped through the bedroom doorway and down the stairs.

Outside, the night was hot and still. Walking into it from the air-conditioned house was like stepping smack into a wool blanket. For a split second, in the dark, I thought I *had* walked into a wool blanket. Mom must have left one hanging on the clothesline. Then I remembered the clothesline was around back. Near the oak tree.

Where my friends were waiting. And why would Mom be drying a heavy wool blanket in the middle of the hottest summer on record?

I hurried into the backyard. The dry grass shone silver in the moonlight. It looked like it had been raining quarters. Real rain would have been nice. It would have made the grass green again.

Flashlights flickered at the edge of the yard. As my eyes adjusted to the moonlight, I saw my teammates gathered beneath the oak tree. The flashlights they held played over the lawn like a swarm of fireflies.

"What's the idea?" I asked, hurrying over.

"We're going to cast a spell," Slingshot said, shrugging off the backpack he wore. Obviously, he was the leader of this operation.

"A spell?" I asked. What, suddenly we were wizards? "What kind of spell?"

"A spell for getting rid of evil spirits," Slingshot said matter-of-factly.

"What evil spirits?"

"Your slump," Slingshot explained.

"My slump is just a slump," I said. "It's terrible, sure. Terrible, rotten, awful, horrible, and just plain lousy. But evil? 'Evil' is too strong a word."

I didn't believe in spells any more than I believed the Easter bunny lived at the North Pole. But not believing was one thing. Striking out five times in a single game was another. It was worse.

"Everybody sit down under the tree and make a circle," Slingshot ordered.

The guys spread out in the moon shadow of the gnarled old tree. When I tried to join the ring, Stump wouldn't let me.

"No way," he said, his Rounders cap pulled low over his eyes. "For the spell to work, you have to sit in the middle of our circle of power."

"Circle of power?" I muttered. "Now I've heard everything. More like a three-ring circus. And you guys are the clowns."

Stump refused to budge, so I had no choice but to scootch into the center of the ring.

Slingshot pulled a thick book out of his pack. After settling it in his lap, he reached into his bag of tricks again and fished out a small silver bottle with a crystal stopper. After that came a handful of those little salt packages you get at Burger Clown and places like that.

"Hurry!" Stump whispered hoarsely. "Midnight is upon us!"

The guys clicked their flashlights under their chins. Their faces blinked on and off in the dark like fritzy lightbulbs. Mr. Bones didn't like it one bit. He ran around trying to lick everyone's pulsating face. The guys gently nudged him away.

"Not now, boy," whispered Slingshot.

Everybody began humming. It sounded like a war chant. Either that or a clogged-up vacuum cleaner.

"Hhmmmm-BA-boom-BAH, hhmmmm-BA-boom-BAH, hhmmmm-BA-boom-BAH."

Between the humming and the flickering lights, things were getting weird.

Really weird.

★ CHAPTER 17 ★

SLINGSHOT OPENED THE book to a marked page. He cleared his throat. The rest of the guys stopped chanting.

"We are gathered here to help the Great Walloper!" Slingshot croaked. He sounded like a frog with a sore throat. "We call upon the powers of Babe Ruth, Hank Aaron, Willie Mays, and all the batting champs who have gone before to vanquish his slump."

"Yeah!" gushed Billy Wishes. "So he can start walloping home runs again."

"Shh!" hissed Ducks.

Slingshot licked his lips and began reading from the book:

"Hot dogs, peanuts, Cracker Jack,
Give our friend his power back!
Bat of wood, horsehide ball,
Knock this slump over the wall!"

Slingshot repeated the charm three times. Then in a booming voice he roared, "Slump, be gone!"

I nearly jumped out of my sneakers, he shouted so loudly.

No one else seemed surprised. They sat as still as snowmen as Slingshot rose and stood over me. Real snowmen would have been nice. They would have been cold. The pitcher ripped open the little envelopes and started dumping salt on my head. A lot of salt. About twenty packets' worth.

"Uh, Slingshot," I said. "That's my head. Not a bowl of popcorn."

"Evil spirits hate salt," Billy Wishes said matter-of-factly.

"Say what?"

Slingshot gave my foot a gentle kick. "Just keep quiet," he said.

"It says so in the book," Gasser explained. "You wouldn't believe all the cool stuff in that book. Slingshot got it out of the library. Like if you mix bats' blood and black toadstools and pour it on someone's shoes, that is a very powerful potion."

"Sure," I said, shaking salt out of my hair. It felt like I'd been turning somersaults on a sandy beach. "Just one cup of it can ruin a perfectly good pair of shoes."

"Funny," said the Glove. "Actually, it will give fits to the person wearing the shoes."

"Fits of anger, probably," I said. "Because you poured gunk on his shoes. Who wouldn't have a fit? They'd be fit to be tied."

"Hey, Walloper. Bad attitude, pal," Ocho said in a huff. "We're doing this to help you."

"Thanks, I guess," I muttered. "Can we go now?"

"First you have to drink the potion," Slingshot said.

Potion? I did not like the sound of that. I did not like it one single bit.

Slingshot handed me the small silver bottle with the crystal stopper.

"Are you serious?"

"Down it in one gulp. Otherwise it won't work." He gave my foot another gentle kick. "Just do it," he hissed.

I took the bottle and looked at it in the beam of a flashlight. A white liquid sloshed around inside. A lot of dark specks floated in the liquid. I gave it a sniff. The smell made my eyes water.

"Here goes nothing," I said.

I raised the bottle to my lips.

You could have heard an ant crack its knuckles. That's how quiet it got under the tree. Everyone was staring at me, waiting to see if I would really down the potion. No one dared to move. I think they forgot to breathe.

I closed my eyes and gulped the speckled white liquid.

"Blecchh!" I gasped. "That was horrible! What in the world was that stuff?"

My friends jumped up and cheered. They laughed and high-fived one another. They slapped me on the back like I had just hit a home run.

"Well," said Slingshot, "the recipe called for hair of a black dog. But we couldn't find a black dog."

"So what did you use instead?" I coughed. Man, that potion was awful. Maybe all potions were awful. I wouldn't recommend them to anyone.

"Well, actually . . ."

Before he could finish, Mr. Bones jumped up

and licked my face.

"Mr. Bones." I laughed. "How could you?" He just licked my face even harder.

Slingshot went on talking. "The recipe also called for foot powder and dragons' blood. We couldn't find any dragons' blood either. So we used hot pepper flakes. You know, the kind they keep in shakers at pizza parlors? We mixed them with milk."

"That was my idea," Billy Wishes said proudly. "Because dragons are really hot."

"Great, Billy," I said. "Just terrific. But what about the foot powder? What in the world did you use for that?"

"Oh," Slingshot shrugged. "We used foot powder. Foot powder is easy to find."

On that note, our little party broke up. Wishing me luck, the guys disappeared into the inky night. I watched their flashlights blink out, unable to tell if the spell had done any good. One thing I did know was that my teammates believed in it. They had done their best to help me. Now the pennant was so close they could taste it, and it was up to me not to disappoint them.

Meanwhile, the only thing I could taste was hot pepper. Hot pepper and foot powder.

★ CHAPTER 18 ★

WHEN I WOKE UP the next morning, my slump was still there. It was so big and black that I bumped my head on it getting out of bed. So much for magic.

"It's no use," I told Mr. Bones. "I just can't shake this thing."

He licked my face gently, then went and stood by the bedroom door and whimpered.

I put on my uniform and banged downstairs for breakfast. My slump knocked against the walls of the staircase on the way down. As if the slump wasn't bad enough, I was also tired from not getting enough sleep. And my breath was really stinky.

"Some spell," I muttered, ducking into the kitchen.

"What's that, son?" Dad asked. He was cooking up one of his famous omelets. Ham, cheese, tomatoes, buttery mushrooms, more cheese.

"Nothing," I said, raising my voice above the blaring music.

Dad liked to blast music when he cooked. He was playing his Game Day get-psyched tunes. That's what we called his CD of sports songs. He often cranked it up before a big game.

"*We will, we will rock you!*" boomed from the speakers.

"Have an omelet," Dad yelled, sliding his creation off the griddle. It was the size of a tube sled. Maybe slightly bigger. A kid could have ridden it down a snowy hill. Snow would have been nice. It would have meant the heat wave was over. My dad was dreaming if he thought I could eat that omelet. Not even Mr. Bones could have finished that whole thing.

Dad used two spatulas to ease the omelet onto a plate, but what he really needed was a crane. The edges flopped over the sides like a tablecloth. He hauled it over to the table. Beneath the plate, the table groaned like it had a broken leg. It was touch and go whether it would stand up to the weight.

Mr. Bones took one look and parked himself beside my chair. He wagged his tail.

Mom came into the kitchen. She sniffed the air. "Oh, yummy," she shouted over the din of the music. She sat down and spread a napkin in her lap. "Your father makes the best omelets," she said.

"Definitely the biggest," I said.

"We will, we will rock you!" boomed the song.

Mr. Bones wagged his tail some more. He loved it when Dad cooked.

"It's a little loud, honey!" Mom shouted.

Dad frowned, but he turned down the volume. He pulled up a chair and carved the omelet like a Thanksgiving turkey. Long strings of gooey cheese stretched from the wedges as he lifted them on to our plates. One summer, my family went to San Francisco on vacation. We drove across the Golden Gate Bridge. Huge cables held it in the air about a million feet above the water. The gooey cheese strings reminded me of the Golden Gate Bridge.

"There's hits in omelets," Dad repeated happily. "This bad boy's good for at least one homer."

I hoped he was right. But I wasn't counting on it. My slump looked worse than ever.

"Which reminds me," said Mom. "I made a banner for the game. What time are you heading to the park?"

"Right after I finish eating," I said between bites.

"Give you a ride?" Dad offered. "It's still hot. Another scorcher."

I shook my head. "No thanks." I had a game-day ritual and I intended to stick to it. Besides, maybe if I rode my bike, my slump would just drift away. Float up into the sky like a lost balloon, disappear forever. "What kind of banner?" I asked Mom.

"You'll just have to wait and see, dear." She winked.

After helping clear the dishes, I said goodbye and headed out into the hot morning with Mr. Bones.

"See you in the second," called my parents from the door. "Good luck, Banjie!"

All the way over to the ballpark, the slump shadowed me and Mr. Bones like a billboard. We couldn't get out from under it no matter how many times we crossed the street. If it had been a billboard, it would have advertised a scary movie: "The Monster Slump. Once it gets you, it never lets go! Now playing in theaters everywhere. Rated A for awful."

The ballpark was packed when Mr. Bones and I got there. Rounders faithful jammed the old yard to bursting. They were going wild.

Punching beach balls around the bleachers. Doing the wave. A real wave would have been nice. It would have carried some water with it.

I headed through the gate with Mr. Bones, then drew up short. Ten feet in front of me stood Gabby Hedron. Head down, she was scribbling in her notebook. She wore a blue Rounders cap. A silver camera dangled from a black strap around her neck. After a second she looked up and our eyes met. Quickly, she looked away and started walking off.

"Gabby!" I called. "Wait!" I had needed to talk to her for a long time.

Screwing up my courage, I hurried to catch her. Mr. Bones got to her first. He leaped up and licked her face, knocking her Rounders cap askew.

"Hi," I said, drawing alongside.

"Walloper," she said.

"Listen," I said.

"Listen," she said.

We both started talking at once. We couldn't hear a word the other was saying.

"Please," I said, holding up my hand. "Let me go first. I've been wanting to say this. I'm sorry for the way I acted the other day. I acted like a jerk. I didn't mean it."

"I'm the one who should say I'm sorry," she said after a second. "I shouldn't have written those stories. I was mad because you made fun of my work."

"But I like your work," I said. "You're the best sports reporter on the paper. I just think it's bad luck to talk about what someone might do before they do it. You know, hit a home run or something. It's like a jinx."

"I never thought of that," she said.

"And I never meant to say those other things," I said. "I was just embarrassed. I don't actually like being the center of attention, you know."

Gabby looked around at the packed ballpark. "It's going to be pretty tough to avoid that now," she pointed out. "What are you going to do?"

"I don't know," I admitted. "I guess I'll just try to do my best. Friends?"

Gabby smiled. "Friends," she agreed.

"I better get in there," I said.

"Go," she said.

I turned to leave.

"Walloper?"

"Yes?"

"Hit one for me!"

I trotted through the gate and onto the field feeling better than I had in a long time, slump or no slump.

★ CHAPTER 19 ★

As I STEPPED OUT onto the field, the guys surrounded me.

"How's the slump, Walloper?" Ocho asked excitedly. "Spell did the trick, right?" He squinted his eyes. "I think it definitely looks smaller."

He was bopping up and down like a kangaroo on a pogo stick. He always bounced when he was excited. I was about to tell him the slump was as fat and awful as ever when Slingshot caught my eye. The lanky pitcher put his finger to his lips.

I looked Ocho in the eye. "I think it is shrinking," I said. "It feels lighter."

"I knew it!" he exclaimed. "I knew the spell would work! In the nick of time, too! We wouldn't stand a chance against those Haymakers with that slump hanging around!"

The guys let out a cheer.

"We've got them now, Walloper," cried Ducks, slapping my back.

"We sure do, Ducks," I said halfheartedly.

"No way we can lose, now your slump's gone," he said happily.

"No way at all." I sighed.

After Ducks wandered off, I sidled up to Slingshot. "What's the big idea?" I hissed. "Everybody seems to think the hocus-pocus stunt you all pulled last night actually worked. Can't they see this thing?"

"Not a big idea at all," Slingshot whispered back. "Pretty small one, really. Sometimes you just gotta believe."

I didn't have time to ask him what *that* meant, because just then Skip Lou called the team together in the dugout, where Mr. Bones sprawled in his usual shady spot under the bench.

"Listen up, fellas," Skip said. "This is the big one. This one is for all the marbles. I want you all to play hard and play fair, just like you always do. If you do that, you'll be winners. No matter what the final score is, you'll be able to hold your heads high. Whichever way the ball bounces out there today, I want you to know that I'm proud of you. Each and every one. Now, let's take it to those Haymakers."

It was a good speech. We knew he meant every word of it. What mattered was not winning or losing. What mattered was how you played the game. But we still wanted to beat Flicker Pringle and those homer-hitting Haymakers. Boy, did we ever want to beat them.

Skip posted the starting lineup on the wall. One by one, we scanned the list to see where he had us batting. After reading it once, I immediately started over again from the top.

My name seemed to be missing.

Slowly and carefully, I looked one more time. Playing third base and batting ninth was Kid Rabbit Winkle. Third base was my position. I always played third base. Always.

But not that day, I didn't. Thanks to that awful slump, I'd been given a new position. One I hadn't played in years. It was called odd man out. I had been bumped. Benched. Scratched. Scrubbed. Sent to ride the pine pony. However you wanted to say it, the meaning was the same. The championship game was on, but I wouldn't be in it.

The news hit me like I had once hit baseballs. It crushed me. As I stood there shaking my head, Skip Lou drew up beside me.

"Sorry, Walloper," he said, patting my shoulder. "I just couldn't risk it. You understand, don't you?"

"Say no more," I said, trying to be brave. "Kid Rabbit has steel springs for pegs and plays third as fine as a fiddle. You made the right call."

I meant what I said. Kid Rabbit was good. Given a chance to start, I knew he'd play like a pair of freshly polished shoes. He would shine. I was truly happy for him. But getting benched still stung.

"Say, Walloper," Skip added kindly. "This way I can always put you in when it really matters. Use you as a pinch hitter with the game on the line."

"In a pinch," I glumly said.

As the Rounders charged onto the field, I joined Mr. Bones in the dugout. My slump hung low under the ceiling, a billowing black mass of whiffs and heartache.

"PLAY BALL!" roared the umpire.

With that, the championship game was on.

Slingshot fired in the first pitch. Powerful Rube Nardley took a vicious cut and missed. Strike one. Two more strikes quickly followed.

"Bush luck, that's all," snarled Rube.

Slingshot didn't pay any attention. He retired the next Haymaker on a grounder to the Glove. Then Flicker Pringle stepped to the plate.

A hush fell over the crowd. They stopped fanning themselves with their scorecards, stopped punching beach balls. A real beach would have been nice. It would have meant cold water. They stopped everything except breathing. And even that they did quietly. It got so still you could hear the toothpick rolling around in Flicker's mouth. He pushed it to one side and said, simply, "Bring it, Slingshot."

Slingshot wound up and delivered. Swinging from his heels, Flicker drove the ball off the wall in deepest center. If you sliced the thinnest thing you could think of in half, a baseball card, say, and then sliced one of the halves in half, that's how close Flicker's bomb came to clearing the wall. You couldn't shave baloney that thin. As he chugged into second with a stand-up double, the expression on his face made a lemon look sweet.

"What's the matter?" called Hanky Burns from the on-deck circle, where he waited to bat.

"Expected a home run," Flicker complained.

Slingshot took the ball and went straight to work. If he was nervous about Flicker dancing off second, he didn't show it. Wasting no time, he blew three hard ones past Hanky.

"Way to go, kid," Skip Lou gushed as Slingshot trotted in from the mound. "You're sharper than old cheese out there."

The only problem was that Flicker Pringle was even sharper. He was a dagger. He struck out Ducks on three high heaters, did the same to Stump, and completely overwhelmed Gasser. Three batters, nine pitches, three strikeouts. His stuff was popping like corn.

In the second inning, Slingshot kept the Haymakers off the bases. When it was our turn to bat, we sent Tugboat, Gilly, and Slingshot to the plate. And Flicker Pringle sent them back in the same order. The tune didn't change in the third. No hits for the Haymakers, and no hits for us.

The game zipped right along. After four innings, Flicker had used up three different catchers on thirty-six blinding strikes. The catchers sat in the dugout nursing hands swollen up to the size of watermelons. Out in the stands, the fans sensed something special in the works and a swoon fell over the park. The place sounded more like a library than a ballpark. It was so hushed, even the peanut vendors whispered. They didn't want to disturb anybody.

Besides, no one was interested in peanuts. They were far too salty and it was far too hot. Only the ice-cream hawkers were doing any business that day, and they had already sold out.

In the fifth, the heat and hard work started to wear on Slingshot. With two outs, he gave up a line-drive double. Then he walked a batter on four wobbly junkers. Two men on. Two men out.

Skip Lou called time and trotted out to the mound. He and Slingshot put their heads together. Kid Rabbit Winkle came in from third and joined the huddle. That's exactly what a third baseman is supposed to do when the manager comes out to jaw with the pitcher. After a minute, the umpire broke up the pow-wow. Skip patted Slingshot on the rump and jogged back to the bench.

"Come on, Slingshot," I hollered. "Get this guy out! You gotta believe!"

The Haymaker at the plate switched his bat like a tiger's tail. The runner on first leaned toward second, the runner on second leaned toward third. Slingshot took a deep breath and fired away. *Crack!* The batter blistered a liner toward left field.

As Kid Rabbit Winkle sprang into the air at third, the breath of a kazillion fans caught in their throats like fish bones. Dirt sprayed from the runners' spikes as they sprinted around the bases. Stretching like a Slinky, Kid Rabbit got a glove on the ball and knocked it down. He bare-handed it and fired to first from his knees.

"OUT!" barked the ump.

It was an impossible play. No one could make that stop. Put Elastic Man at third, and he couldn't stretch long enough to intercept that line drive. Fire the ball from a howitzer and it wouldn't get to first in time. But Kid Rabbit did it.

We went into the bottom of the fifth still tied at nothing.

Flicker Pringle came out nastier than ever. Hurling darts, BBs, bullets, and missiles, he again fanned our side on nine pitches. Forget about touching his stuff. We couldn't even get within shouting distance.

In the sixth, Slingshot got the lead-off hitter to wave at a curveball in the dirt for strike three, then gave up two singles and a walk. The air went out of the stadium like a flat tire. The only sound was the steady *plop, plop, plop* of sweat dripping from a thousand sunburned foreheads onto hard wooden bleachers.

With the bases loaded, burly Hoot Fewster, the Haymakers' mountain of a first baseman, stepped up to bat. He cocked his bat over his shoulder and waited for the pitch. He knew Slingshot was spent. One swing and he could blow the game wide-open.

Slingshot dug deep and came up with the best pitch he could find: a loopy curve. Hoot smirked as he cranked it high over the head of Ocho in right field. The three base runners took off instantly, tearing for home. Ocho turned and raced after the ball. Two steps from the wall, he got under it and made an over-the-shoulder catch. Somehow, he stayed on his feet. In one fluid motion, he turned and fired the ball to Gilly at first. The runner was already halfway home. Gilly fielded the throw on one hop and stepped on the bag for a game-saving double play.

Everybody started breathing again.

Into the last of the sixth we went, nothing but zeroes on the scoreboard. Flicker stormed back out to the mound, hotter and smokier than ever. As far as he was concerned, the Haymakers should have been leading by five or six runs by now. It completely cheesed him that our defense had kept them from scoring. An angry Flicker Pringle was a terrible thing. He made Ocho and the Glove pay for their web gems by twisting them into human pretzels. Strikes one, two, three, and four, five, six.

In other words, he was three strikes away

from pitching the first perfect "perfect" game in the history of baseball. Seventeen Rounders had gone up to face him; seventeen Rounders had fanned. All on three-pitch strikeouts.

We were one out away from making history.

The wrong kind of history.

In the broiling stands, fans fainted from tension.

In the dugout, Skip Lou looked up and down the bench. What he saw did not please him. Our guys were gassed. We looked beaten. We were hot and tired and overmatched by Flicker Pringle. No one had touched the guy all day, and no one looked hopeful now. Skip's gaze settled on me. Ever so slightly, he nodded.

"Get in there, Walloper," he said slowly. "Get in there and wallop us a pinch-hit dinger."

I could hardly believe it. Down to the last out of the last inning, with the pennant on the line and my slump looming like an overgrown gorilla, he wanted me to go in there and break up the first perfect "perfect" game in the history of baseball?

"You sure, Skip?" I asked.

"I'm sure," he said. "We can't send Slingshot out there for extra innings. His arm will fall off. We've got to end this thing now."

"BATTER UP!" called the umpire.

★ CHAPTER 20 ★

As I ROSE FROM the bench, Mr. Bones leaped up and used his tongue like a paintbrush on my face.

"Thanks, pal," I said. "I needed that."

Billy Wishes handed me my favorite game bat, a polished Louisville Slugger.

"Did you give it some elbow grease?" I asked.

"Even better," he grinned. "I've been sleeping with it under my bed since Lumleyville."

I gave his head a pat for extra luck and clattered up the dugout steps.

"Hey, Walloper," he called to my back. "Blast one to the moon!"

On the short walk to the plate, my slump seemed to deepen and darken. It filled the stadium like darkness fills the night, completely blocking out the sun. Such gloom was cast upon the field that the groundskeeper turned on the stadium lights.

I stepped into the box and waggled my bat. I tried to feel brave.

Out on the mound, Flicker stamped the dirt. His slitted eyes glowed in the strange twilight like the orbs of some kind of demon, smoky and hot. Way out in the bleachers, a single fan rose and broke the tense silence that had settled over the ballpark. She waved a big cardboard sign over her head. The sign had a target painted on it in red and white. The words underneath said HIT IT HERE!

It was my mom. My dad was at her side. They still believed.

Fans sitting near them read the sign and began to cheer.

"Hit it here! Hit it here!" they chanted. The

cry spread through the stands like wildfire. Soon everyone in the park was standing and chanting. They all believed.

The noise didn't bother Flicker Pringle one bit. He rolled the toothpick around in his mouth, reared back, and flung an aspirin. I tried to swing, but the bat got caught up over my shoulder and I couldn't bring it around in time.

"Oomph," wheezed the catcher.

"STEE-RIKE ONE!" cried the umpire.

"What happened?" I asked.

"Bat snagged on your slump, kid," the ump said. "Try swinging lower."

Flicker wound up and delivered smoke.

"Yeeow," cried the catcher.

"STEE-RIKE TWO!" roared the umpire.

"Where was it?" I asked. "Because I sure never saw it."

"Neither did I," admitted the ump. "But it had to be a strike. Every other one was."

We were all the way up against the wall

now. Bottom of the sixth, nobody on, two outs, two strikes. In the dugout, the guys turned their hats inside out and wore them rally style. They still believed.

I called time and stepped out of the box. Glancing into the stands, I caught sight of Gabby sitting with the other reporters in the third-base boxes. Our eyes met. She leaned out of her seat and flashed the thumbs-up sign. She still believed.

I took a deep breath and stepped back into the box. The crowd started chanting again. "Hit it here! Hit it here!" They still believed.

As Flicker brought his hands together high over his head, the air was so hot and heavy you could have cut patches out of it and sold them as blankets to Eskimos.

He wheeled and launched a comet.

This time I didn't bother looking for the ball. I just trusted my instincts and tried to believe in my talent. Maybe I was beginning to understand what Slingshot meant. Maybe faith is all you've got sometimes. Sometimes, you just have to believe. I closed my eyes and listened for the *whoosh*. When it sounded right, I swung with all the mustard I could muster.

The crack was like nothing ever heard on Earth. It was deep as thunder and sharp as lightning. The ball flew off my bat like it had wings.

On the way to center field, the ball punched a hole clean through the low, dark cloud of my slump. I was halfway to first when the first fat raindrops began to fall.

The ball cleared the wall and showed no sign of slowing. The farther it soared, the harder the rain fell. It laced down in buckets, sheets, torrents, cataracts, rivers. By the time I tagged second, water sloshed up to my ankles. Getting to third was more like swimming than running.

The ball left Rambletown city limits and headed for the county line, dragging a string of thunderheads as it flew. It soared above farms and forests, unleashing rain that watered fields and filled entire lakes. All across the country, cows came out of barns and opened their mouths to the sky, and pigs wallowed in oceans of fresh mud. The corn turned green and shot up six feet.

Rounding third, I paused to tip my hat to the rocking grandstand. Fans were going crazy. In the middle of it all, Mom and Dad bounced up and down like they were on springs, Mom's sign turning to paste in the downpour. Then I dived into the flood and did the backstroke all the way home, where Mr. Bones doggie-paddled in circles and my teammates leaped and splashed and Gabby snapped one picture after another, her flash popping like lightning in the rainstorm.

My slump was over.

The Rambletown Rounders had beaten the Hog City Haymakers.

We had won the pennant. Finally, we were champs.

And somewhere, somehow that ball was still

going, streaking across the sky like a shooting star. One day in the future, a little green spaceman might be standing up on Mars, and he might look out and see a new planet spinning his way. A tiny white planet with little red stitches. That's how far the old baseball traveled. All the way into deepest space.

Cross my heart and hope to die.

LINEUP OF THE RAMBLETOWN ROUNDERS

Ducks Bunion, left field; throws left, bats left; .301 BA

Stump Plumwhiff, shortstop; throws right, bats right; .280 BA

The Great Walloper, Banjo H. Bishbash, third base; throws right, bats right; .560 BA

Gasser Phipps, center field; throws right, bats right; .305 BA

Tugboat Tooley, catcher; throws right, bats right; .277 BA

Gilly Wishes, first base; throws left, bats left; .309 BA

Slingshot Slocum, pitcher; throws right, bats right; .333 BA

Octavio "Ocho" James, right field; throws right, bats right; .286 BA

Ellis "the Glove" Rodriguez, second base; throws right, bats right; .304 BA

Kid Rabbit Winkle, substitute third
    base; throws right, bats right;
    .299 BA
Skipper Lou "Skip-to-My-Lou"
    Clementine, manager

REVISED ROUNDERS' LINEUP FOR THE FINAL
    GAME VS. THE HOG CITY HAYMAKERS
    Ducks Bunion, left field, lh
    Stump Plumwhiff, shortstop, rh
    Gasser Phipps, center field, rh
    Tugboat Tooley, catcher, rh
    Gilly Wishes, first base, lh
    Slingshot Slocum, pitcher, rh
    Octavio "Ocho" James, right field, rh
    Ellis "the Glove" Rodriguez, second
        base, rh
    Kid Rabbit Winkle, third base, rh
    The Great Walloper, Banjo H.
        Bishbash, pinch hitter, rh
    Skipper Lou "Skip-to-My-Lou"
        Clementine, manager

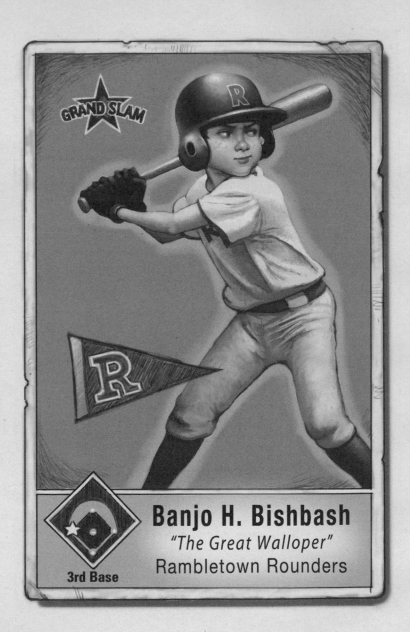

GRAND SLAM

Banjo H. Bishbash
"The Great Walloper"
Rambletown Rounders

3rd Base

Q&A with Kevin Markey

Kevin Markey's Fantasy Baseball Picks

Kevin Markey's Top Ten Moments in Baseball History

Q&A with Kevin Markey

How did you get the idea to write about Walloper and the Rounders?

I wrote *Slumpbuster* for my nephew Brendan, a great reader who was just beginning to play organized baseball. Brendan has since blossomed into an all-star player and he continues to read like crazy.

Baseball offers such terrific material: action, excitement, colorful characters, funny nicknames. Every game is a story, and a whole season of games is like an epic saga. You can't beat baseball as a subject.

Slumpbuster is full of jokes. How do you come up with them? When you're writing, how do you know what's funny?

Brendan and my own kids serve as my perfect audience. I ask myself: What do these guys like? What makes them laugh? When I hear them giggling in my head, I know I'm on the right track.

A big part of the Super Sluggers is the language Walloper uses, the way he always compares one thing to another. Part of the inspiration for that comes from baseball's rich tradition of colorful words and expressions: Fastballs are "high cheese" and an old-style round catcher's mitt is a "pie plate." Players constantly come up with metaphors like "trying to hit that high cheese was harder than drinking coffee with a fork." Great stuff, if you like words.

Did you play baseball as a kid?

I played Little League, but definitely was no Walloper! Far from blasting homers, I was more likely to draw a walk, steal second, steal third, and come home on a wild pitch. Most of the pitchers I faced were kind of wild, so the strategy worked pretty well. I very clearly remember my first-ever hit. The ball soared over the shortstop's head, dropped between the left fielder and center fielder (who nearly collided), and rolled all the way to the edge of the woods behind the field at Nathan Bill Park in Springfield, Massachusetts. I was so surprised I nearly forgot to run.

What's so great about baseball?

Baseball's great because it's full of twists and turns and joy and sorrow and you never know what's going to happen next. Even when things turn out badly, you can still have hope. As Brooklyn Dodgers fans used to say, "Wait till next year."

Why are you such a diehard Red Sox fan?

I'm a Sox fan because I was lucky enough to grow up in New England at a time when Boston fielded some really exciting teams. My first great fan memory is of Carlton Fisk winning Game 6 of the 1975 World Series for the Boston Red Sox: his famous body-

language homer off the left field foul pole in the bottom of the twelfth against Cincinnati at Fenway Park. I'm forever grateful my parents let my brothers and me stay up WAY past bedtime to watch that game. After that, I was hooked.

In your opinion, who is the greatest baseball player of all time?

I think the only possible answer is Babe Ruth. His towering homers and matching personality completely changed the game. Statistically, the Babe dominates. He's at or near the top of the all-time list in every offensive category, including slugging percentage, on-base percentage, and, of course, home runs. In a twenty-year career, he made it to the World Series ten times, and his teams won seven championships. You know what else is incredible? The Babe stole home ten times. Sure, he may look roly-poly in old photographs and film clips, but in his prime the dude was *fast*! Plus, before he set all his batting records, he was a total stud pitcher. His winning percentage ranks among the very best in history.

What's with the Yankees–Red Sox rivalry?

Boston and New York have two very old, very good teams with huge and passionate fan bases. And because they're both in the American League East, year after year they've got to beat each other to win the title. All that shared history adds up. Fans remember the joy or heartbreak of every last game. For Red Sox fans, emotions are further stoked by decades where the Yankees came out on top of the rivalry. All that winning gave them a lot of confidence—arrogance, you might say—and it drove us crazy. Over the last few seasons, the Sox have won a couple of World Series titles. Now Yankees fans know how we felt all those years. Their passion to get back on top makes the rivalry more intense than ever.

Kevin Markey's Fantasy Baseball Picks

Egads, can it be true? Does my twenty-one-man roster (positional starters, eight pitchers, five-man bench) really feature as many Yankees as Red Sox? Afraid so: Rivera and Jeter just can't be overlooked. But, hey, this is only fantasy. In real life, I'll take the full Boston lineup any day.

Catcher: Joe Mauer, Minnesota Twins
First Base: Albert Pujols, St. Louis Cardinals
Second Base: Chase Utley, Philadelphia Phillies
Third Base: Evan Longoria, Tampa Bay Rays
Shortstop: Hanley Ramirez, Florida Marlins
Right Field: Matt Kemp, Los Angeles Dodgers
Center Field: Jacoby Ellsbury, Boston Red Sox
Left Field: Carl Crawford, Tampa Bay Rays

Bench
Infield: Ryan Howard, Philadelphia Phillies; Derek Jeter, New York Yankees; Prince Fielder, Milwaukee Brewers
Outfield: Ryan Braun, Milwaukee Brewers; Ichiro Suzuki, Seattle Mariners

Starting Pitchers: Tim Lincecum, San Francisco Giants; Roy Halladay, Toronto Blue Jays; Adam Wainwright, St. Louis Cardinals; Justin Verlander, Detroit Tigers; Jon Lester, Boston Red Sox
Relievers: Mariano Rivera, New York Yankees; Joe Nathan, Minnesota Twins; Huston Street, Colorado Rockies

Kevin Markey's Top Ten Moments
in Baseball History

Robinson Breaks Color Barrier
Jackie Robinson joins the Brooklyn Dodgers on April 15, 1947, becoming the first African-American player in Major League Baseball.

The Shot Heard Round the World
With two on and two out in the ninth inning of the 1951 National League playoffs, the New York Giants trail the Brooklyn Dodgers 4–2. Bobby Thomson steps up and homers, winning the game—and the pennant—for the Giants.

Maz's World Series Walk-Off
Pittsburgh's Bill Mazeroski leads off the bottom of the ninth of Game 7 of the 1960 World Series with a home run, breaking a 9–9 tie and lifting the Pirates to the championship over the Yankees.

Larsen's Perfect Game
On October 8, 1956, Yankee Don Larsen pitches the first perfect game in World Series history. More than fifty years later, he's still the only guy to have done it.

Fisk Waves the Ball Fair
Carlton Fisk wins Game 6 of the 1975 World Series for the Red Sox by homering off the left field foul pole

at Fenway Park in the bottom of the twelfth inning.

The Babe Calls His Shot

In the fifth inning of the 1932 World Series between the Yankees and the Cubs, Babe Ruth points his bat toward the center field bleachers at Wrigley Field, then smashes the very next pitch over the wall. This one has been debated ever since it happened. Some people say Ruth merely might have pointed at Chicago pitcher Charley Root. But I like to believe the Babe really called his shot. Once I was lucky enough to meet Ruth's granddaughter Linda Ruth Tosetti and ask her about the famous incident. She told me her parents talked about it all the time when she was a kid and they knew for a fact the story was true. "The Chicago fans and players had been riding my grandfather hard all day," she said. "He was tired of it. Chicago pitcher Charley Root threw a pitch for strike one. My grandfather looked at the bench and held up one finger. Root threw strike two. My grandfather held up two fingers. Then he raised his bat and pointed at the bleachers. Which is exactly where he put the next pitch." Good enough for me.

The Catch

In the eighth inning of Game 1 of the 1954 World Series, Willie Mays of the New York Giants chases down a fly ball by Cleveland's Vic Wertz in deep center field of the Polo Grounds. His amazing over-the-shoulder catch preserves a 2–2 tie; New York goes on to win the game in 10 innings and the Series in a sweep.

The Mad Dash
Seventh and deciding game of the 1946 World Series between Boston and St. Louis, score tied at three with two outs in the bottom of the eighth. Enos "Country" Slaughter stands on first base for the Cardinals. When teammate Harry Walker raps a line drive to right, Slaughter takes off running and doesn't stop until he gets all the way home—just ahead of the tag. Cardinals win the game and the Series.

Clemente Hits 3,000th in Final At Bat
Roberto Clemente of the Pittsburgh Pirates doubles off the Mets' Jon Matlack in the final game of the 1972 season for his 3,000th career hit. A few months later, Clemente is killed in a plane crash while traveling to Nicaragua to help earthquake victims.

Hubbell Fans the Hall of Fame
Pitcher Carl Hubbell of the New York Giants strikes out Babe Ruth, Lou Gehrig, Jimmie Foxx, Al Simmons, and Joe Cronin one after another during the first and second innings of the 1934 All-Star Game.

An excerpt from

Springtime in Rambletown means one thing—another season of Rounders baseball! But this year, old man winter has delivered more snow than the post office has delivered mail. As the team tries to "warm up" for the upcoming season, they welcome a new center fielder: Orlando Ramirez. He makes one spectacular grab after another . . . before smashing into the outfield wall like a crash test dummy! Orlando and the Rounders will need a miracle—or a really big shovel—to put the brakes on Orlando's collision course with the wall and this never-ending cold spell.

The next day was balmy. Almost tropical. The temperature got all the way up to freezing, and it didn't snow more than a foot or so.

Mr. Bones and I bundled into our winter gear. I grabbed my bat and my mitt and my shovel. We headed over to the ballpark. Today we were going to practice hitting. Hopefully, it would go better than yesterday's fielding.

Orlando was digging out the bases with the rest of the guys when Mr. Bones and I arrived. The town plows were again doing their best to make the outfield playable.

11

EXTRAS

Mr. Bones ran right over and licked Orlando's face.

"How's the old bean, Orlando?" I asked. Meaning his noggin. Calabash. Pumpkin.

You know, his head.

"Rock solid," he said. "Never better."

"Glad to hear it," I told him. "The wall looks pretty good too. I see it's still standing where you tried to knock it down."

I patted him on the shoulder to let him know I was just kidding.

Orlando smiled.

We cleared the field of the fresh snow.

"Spring is in the air," said Lou "Skip-to-My-Lou" Clementine.

"Sure it is," said Slingshot as he walked out to the mound. "It is somewhere. Just not here. Australia, maybe."

"Only six days until we take on those Hog City Haymakers," said Skip. "Cold and snowy or warm and sunny, it doesn't matter. In less than a week we finally play baseball."

Tugboat pulled his catcher's mask over his ski hat and crouched down behind home plate. Slingshot tossed him a few easy ones. Tugboat caught them and fired them back.

"Batter up," called Skip Lou.

That was me.

Billy Wishes handed me my favorite bat. A big, long, heavy Louisville Slugger. I rubbed the batboy's head for luck and stepped up to the plate.

"Nice and easy, Slingshot," said Skip.

The pitcher nodded and threw me a fat one right down the middle.

I gave it a clout. The bat buzzed in my hands like a swarm of angry bees.

"Yowza!" I bleated as the ball sailed foul and buried itself in a snowdrift down the left field line. I wasn't used to hitting in cold weather. It stung.

I called time-out and pulled a pair of puffy winter mittens over my thin batting gloves. Then I stepped up to the plate again. Slingshot

13

tossed me another cream pie.

This time I really clobbered it. The bat still buzzed, but the mittens softened the pain from a furious sting to more of a fuzzy vibration. The ball soared into the outfield.

Deep center.

Orlando locked onto its flight and gave chase. Ten feet in front of the sturdy wooden fence, his path crossed that of the ball. He took wing and snapped it up in his glove midair like a bat devouring a mosquito.

Amazing catch! Highlight material. It should have been on SportsCenter.

Orlando landed on his feet.

He did not fall down.

But he didn't stop either.

He couldn't.

"Uh-oh," I said, hoping lightning wouldn't strike twice.

I held my breath. I closed my eyes.

Sha-bam!

Lightning struck twice. Rather, Orlando did.

He slammed into the wall like a football player trying to barrel into the end zone.

The wall made like the Pittsburgh Steelers defense. It didn't budge an inch.

When the reverberations finally died down and the frozen earth stopped trembling, we ran out to check on Orlando. He lay on the ground not more than three feet from where he'd crashed the day before. Mr. Bones got there first. He licked Orlando's face. He wagged his tail and licked some more.

"Pfft!" said Orlando.

He sat up and scratched Mr. Bones behind his ears.

"Orlando," I said, puffing onto the scene. "We held ten bake sales and six car washes to raise the money to get this wall built. If you knock it down, we'll never get another. Are you all right?"

"I've taken bigger lumps falling out of bed," he said.

He got up and opened his glove. Nesting

inside like a big, round egg was the ball.

If Orlando didn't knock himself goofy, he was going to be a really great center fielder.

Slowly, we all started walking back across the field.

"How about Two Time?" suggested Tugboat. "On account of this is the second time he ran into the wall."

"Greased Pig," said Ducks. "Because he skitters all over the place like a greased pig at a country fair."

"Banana Peel."

"Wallbanger."

"Wrecking Ball."

"Superstar," said Billy Wishes. "On account of he makes super catches, then he sees stars when he runs into the wall."

We all stopped walking.

"Not bad," said the Glove. "Not bad at all."

Everyone agreed that Superstar had a certain ring to it.

But somehow it still wasn't quite right.

"A player can be a superstar," said Ocho. "And Orlando definitely can run and catch with the best of them. But can Superstar really be a nickname?"

"It's like I told you," Orlando said glumly. "No one has ever been able to pin a good one on me."

"Don't worry," we promised. "We'll come up with a winner if it's the last thing we do."

One by one, we slapped Orlando on the back.

"Take it easy," we warned before scattering across the hard-frozen field to our own positions.

Ducks stepped up to the plate. Slingshot lobbed one easy pitch after another right over the middle of the plate. Ducks swung as if the ball was a piñata and if he smacked it hard enough it would split open and spill candy. He didn't manage to shatter any of Slingshot's batting practice tosses, but he did turn them around in a hurry. He lasered shots all over the field.

EXTRAS

Then it was Gilly's turn. He too teed off on one fat pitch after another.

We all hit the ball pretty well. It was good to see the winter layoff hadn't damaged our swings.

Fielding was another story. All practice long, we struggled to catch the ball. We tripped and slipped and stumbled. None of us had much success staying upright. But no one had a harder time than Orlando. The kid from Florida ran down every long ball to center. And he plowed into the wall after every catch. He never dropped a single fly. But by the end of practice the wall looked like French toast. Battered.

And so was Orlando.